from
CALEB'S
COLORS

●●●

"You wish to touch the painting," said Prax. It wasn't so much a question as a statement of fact. "You may do so. These paintings are meant to be touched."

I reached out toward one of those redder-than-red leaves to feel its velvet texture . . .

. . . and when I drew my hand away, I was holding the leaf between my fingers!

I gasped, and let the leaf flutter to the ground.

Prax smiled. "The task of the artist," he said, "is the creation of worlds. Very few succeed. Many die trying."

Also by Neal Shusterman

Novels:

Scorpion Shards*
The Eyes of Kid Midas*
Dissidents*
The Shadow Club
Speeding Bullet
What Daddy Did

Non-Fiction

Kid Heroes*

Story Collections

MINDTWISTERS: Stories to Shred Your Head*
MINDSTORMS: Stories to Blow Your Mind*
Darkness Creeping
Darkness Creeping II

*Published by Tor Books

MIND QUAKES

STORIES TO SHATTER YOUR BRAIN

90821

Neal Shusterman

A TOM DOHERTY ASSOCIATES BOOK
NEW YORK

MINDQUAKES: STORIES TO SHATTER YOUR BRAIN

Copyright © 1996 by Neal Shusterman

Cover art by Robert Papp

A Tor Book
Published by Tom Doherty Associates, Inc.
175 Fifth Avenue
New York, NY 10010

Tor® is a registered trademark of Tom Doherty Associates, Inc.

ISBN: 0-812-55197-4

First edition: May 1996

Printed in the United States of America

0   9   8   7   6   5   4   3   2

Dedication

*This
book is
dedicated to
my teachers: Hertha
Paustian, who challenged
me to write a story a week in
ninth grade; Randy Perrezini, who
gave me the* Collected Stories of John
Cheever; *Gilbert Weatherby, who left too
soon; Lori Aguera-Arcas, who taught me how
to paint a canvas of possibilities; and Oakley Hall,
who gave me the confidence to write that first novel, and
reminded me that even the pyramids began with a single stone.*

Acknowledgments

Many thanks to all the movers and shakers who helped create *MindQuakes*. Thanks to Peggy Black, and the students at Longfellow, Irving, and Whittier Middle Schools in Norman, Oklahoma, for their contribution to *Yardwork*. Thanks to my sons Brendan and Jarrod, for their undying fascination with a certain Scottish Monster. Thanks to Elaine, who shares with me the joys of life, and listens to all of my ideas—even the dumb ones. Thanks to Terry Black, for whom I wrote *Dead Letter*, and whose formidable writing talents rest in fertile soil (but usually not for long). Thanks to Sean Ponce, whose labors inspired *Retaining Walls*.

And my deepest gratitude to Kathleen Doherty, Jonathan Schmidt, and everyone at Tor Books for their remarkable persistence of vision!

N. S.

CONTENTS

• •

YARDWORK

. . . .

As I step outside, a strange feeling tugs at my spine. Perhaps that's what it feels like when you first step into a nightmare.

Don't be silly, Jeremy, I tell myself, *there's nothing to be afraid of.*

Today the wind has brought an unpleasant smell sweeping across the neighborhood. It's tinged with a slight scent of fertilizer.

The smell's coming from Mr. Jackson's house. My mom told me all about Mr. Jackson—how he used to live here before I was born. How he spent most of his life in that house; how his beautiful garden had been the envy of the neighborhood.

He had a family, but no one knows what happened to them. They left, he left soon after, and the garden just died.

By the time I was born, the house was an ugly blotch on our

neighborhood. People would live there for only a few months before leaving, and then it became completely abandoned. Now it was covered with graffiti and filled with broken, boarded-up windows. It bothered me to have a place like that next door, but like anything, I got used to it.

Then last week, Mr. Jackson just came back, like he'd never left. Since then, I've been watching the house . . . and watching him. The house hasn't changed—he hasn't had anyone come to fix the windows or paint over the graffiti. All he does is work in his garden. He sure loves that garden.

Now, as I step outside, I can hear him back there. I can hear the *skitch . . . brummp, skitch . . . brummp* of his little trowel digging up the dirt and throwing it over his shoulder. I know he's planting more flowers. Until Mr. Jackson came back, there weren't any flowers in *that* garden. Nothing grew there but ugly weeds that got filled with torn rags, Kleenex, and candy wrappers. Whatever the wind brought to our neighborhood got snagged in the thick weeds of that abandoned backyard and stayed there.

Until last week, that is. That's when Mr. Jackson showed up and began hacking those weeds, putting them into trash bags, and hauling them out to the curb. The weeds are all gone now, and bit by bit that wasteland of a yard is filling with flowers.

"Jeremy, don't go bothering the man," my mom had told me. But what she really means is "Stay away from him, Jeremy, because he's not quite right. Leave him to his business, and maybe when his business is done he'll leave forever and they'll tear that ugly house down."

But Mom's asleep on the couch now, so she doesn't have to know, and I can't resist the curiosity itching at my brain. It's a few minutes after dark. A night chill has set in, and the sun is long gone, leaving a ribbon of blue on the horizon that's fading fast. I stand at the edge of our property, peering at the upstairs windows of the old house, nervously running my fingers through my hair. Boards have covered most of those windows for years now, and thick spiderwebs fill the space between the boards.

Taking a deep breath, I cross over, through the gaping hole in the old wooden fence, into the world of Mr. Jackson. Here that dark and earthy fertilizer smell is stronger. There are no lights on in the house. I don't think Mr. Jackson has had the electricity turned back on.

He's back there all right, doing his yardwork—I can see his shadow now as I make my way down the side of the house toward the backyard. I can see that shadow on hands and knees in the dirt.

Skitch . . . brummp, skitch . . . brummp.

Holding on to a rusty old drainpipe snaking down the edge of the house, I round the corner to see him in the light of the half moon. He's setting a fresh row of flowers in the growing garden. I can't tell what they are, because all I can see is black and white.

"Are those zinnias you're planting?" I ask, remembering that my mom liked to grow zinnias.

He doesn't look up at me. I figure he's too deaf to hear me—and good thing too. I've got no business here. I can just go back home, turn on the TV, and forget Mr. Jackson; no one would be the wiser. But then he speaks in a soft whisper of a voice that sounds filled with gravel and wrapped in cotton.

"Marigolds," he says. "Man-in-the-moon marigolds, they are."

Skitch . . . brummp. He plants one more, then finally turns to look at me. I don't see his eyes, just dark shadows where they should be.

"You the Harrison boy?" he asks.

I nod, then say "Yes," figuring he can't see my nod in the dark.

"I see you lookin' out your window at me," he says. "Am I putting on a good show for you here?"

"It's not like that," I try to explain. "I've just been wondering why you're . . . I mean, look at the house. What's so important about the yard when the house looks like hell?"

"How would *you* know what hell looks like?" he asks me. *Skitch . . . brummp.* Dirt flies over his shoulder, and in goes another marigold.

By now I'm feeling all tongue-twisted and bone cold, and fear is clawing at my gut. I grip that cold drainpipe as if it can give me some comfort, and it comes loose in my hands.

Yelping, I fall to the ground, right into the bed of flowers.

"I'm sorry," I stammer, scrambling to my feet, wishing I was anywhere else in the world. When I look down, I shudder at the sight of the imprint I made in the flowers. The way the moon's casting shadows tonight, I can see the shape of my whole body, as if I'm still lying down.

I figure the old man is going to have a fit and start scooping out my brains with his planting trowel, or bury his little hand rake in the side of my neck, but he doesn't. Instead he just looks down at the crushed flowers.

"Those're no good anymore," he says calmly. "I gotta put in all new ones now."

He looks at me, and now I can see his eyes. They are ancient, the lids almost closing over them in tired sags of skin.

"I don't need you here,' he tells me in that gravel-cotton voice. "I can do this myself. I don't need you."

Well, I don't need a second invitation to leave. I step back, stumbling over the broken drainpipe, and tear out of the yard, through the hole in the wooden fence and back onto my own property where the moon doesn't seem to shine quite as coldly.

I can't sleep that night, because I hear him through my closed window. Only now do I realize that he doesn't sleep—he works all through the night in that garden. *What is it about that garden?* I wonder as I lay awake. *Why is it so important to him?*

When the sun comes up in the morning, I drag myself out of bed and peer out the window. In the light of day, the garden doesn't look quite so creepy. In fact, it looks kind of pretty and peaceful. Rows of flowers of all different colors surround a single open patch of dirt. I wonder what he's going to put there.

Downstairs, I force myself to drink Mom's coffee so that I can stay awake. "I think Mr. Jackson's going to put a fountain in the middle of his garden," I tell my mom as she tosses a couple of waffles on my plate. "What do you think?"

"His business is his business," Mom says. But what she really means is *"I don't want you to go sticking your nose in that garden."* Mom's always been a mind-your-own kind of person.

"Lock the door when you leave," she tells me, like she always does when she heads off for work. Like if she didn't I'd leave the door wide open.

As I eat, I can hear the rattle of a wheelbarrow next door. Mr. Jackson's busy with his endless yardwork. I'm about to leave for school, but before I do, I get an idea. You see, I'm not quite as mind-your-own as Mom is.

In a couple of minutes, I leave the house, but instead of turning right and heading toward school, I turn left and slip through the hole in the wooden fence.

Mr. Jackson is where I knew I'd find him, in the corner of the yard, turning up the earth for a new batch of flowers and tossing the bigger stones into the wheelbarrow. He wears a long-sleeved shirt, buttoned all the way to the top, even though the day is hot. His hands are covered with dirt and they're just as leathery and wrinkled as the skin on his face.

"I . . . I thought you might like some breakfast," I tell him. I hold the plate toward him. "Waffles. I didn't know if you liked syrup, so I put it in a little cup on the side, see?"

Still across the yard, he stands there looking at me like he's looking through a wall. Then he slowly makes his way toward me, careful not to trample his flowers with his heavy work boots. His feet drag as he moves, as if he's got no muscles in them—as if he's pulling his legs up from the seat of his pants like one of those marionettes. He reaches out and takes the plate and cup from me.

"Thank you," he says simply, then puts the waffles down on a cinder block and reaches into his pocket, handing me a wad of crumpled dollar bills.

I shake my head, not wanting to take the money, and, for that matter, not wanting to touch that dirty, puffy hand. "No," I tell him, "no, you don't have to pay me—the waffles are my treat—to make up for messing up your flowers last night." When I look down, I see that he's already replanted the area.

He shakes his head slowly. "I'm not paying you," he tells me. "I'm asking you to do something for me." He clears his throat. It crackles like eggshells breaking. "I was wrong," he says. "Last night I was wrong. I *do* need someone to help me. You understand?"

I shrug. "Sure. What do you want me to do?"

"Flowers from the nursery. Lots of flowers."

"What kind?"

He thinks about that for a moment, then smiles, revealing just a sparse scattering of rotten teeth. I have to cast my eyes down because I can't look at that terrible mouth.

"Any kind you like," he tells me. "Pick your favorites . . . and buy a shovel," he says before I go, "a bigger shovel."

After school, I head right out to the nursery with the old wagon I used when I was a little kid. I don't know much about flowers, but I pick out a few trays of really nice ones for Mr. Jackson's garden. Then I pull it all home in the rusty old wagon and present it to Mr. Jackson.

"Help me plant them," he says.

I look at my watch. Mom won't be home for another hour. I've got no homework, so I figure, Sure, why not. No good deed goes unrewarded, right? Anyway, I head for the patch of dirt in the middle of the yard that definitely needs some color when Mr. Jackson shouts: "No!"

It nearly makes me jump out of my skin. Then he quickly changes his tone. "No, not there."

"Oh, right," I say. "I forgot about the fountain. It *is* going to be a fountain, right?"

But he doesn't answer me. He just directs me to a far corner with my trays of plants.

For a few minutes we work quietly, but my mind gets to working overtime. I start wondering about that patch of dirt. Not what's going on top of it, but what's underneath. I start wondering how deep this garden is planted.

"Mr. Jackson, whatever happened to your family?"

He plants three geraniums before answering in his gravelly toothless voice. "People break apart sometimes" is all he says.

I think of my own parents. Once my parents got divorced I saw less and less of my father until I didn't see him at all. Maybe I'll never see him again, I don't know. *People break apart.* I imagine my own dad fifty years from now, an old man in a garden. No way to find him; no way to talk to him even if I do find him. Just the thought of it makes me plant the flowers faster and faster, trying to drive the thought out of my mind.

"Your family didn't go with you when you left here?" I ask, unable to keep my fool mouth shut.

"Nope. There were just old folks where I went," says Mr. Jackson. "Old folks, nurses, and more old folks."

"Did they treat you okay," I ask, realizing that he must have been in a retirement home.

Mr. Jackson thinks about it. "They cared for me, which is about the best I can say for them." Then he stops planting for a moment. "They cared for me," he says again, "but that wasn't home. *This* is. You understand?"

I glance over at the bald spot in the center of the yard again. "What's over there, Mr. Jackson? Is there something . . . under the dirt?"

"Nothing," he tells me. "Nothing but worms."

The light is growing dim now. I listen for the sound of my mother's car. Above us I can see large birds circling. Vultures. I can't remember seeing them in our neighborhood before.

Then I hear Mr. Jackson grunt, and when I look up, something awful has happened. He was digging with his little trowel and somehow slit his right arm, leaving a gash as wide as all outdoors—at least four or five inches.

"That's not good," says Mr. Jackson, in the same calm voice he used when I fell in his flowers last night.

"I'll go call a doctor!" I shout, but as I start to take off, he yells: "No! No doctors."

"But your arm."

"It's *my* arm and *I'll* deal with it."

He grabs a dirty rag from his back pocket, and I catch sight of the words stenciled on it. It reads DADE COUNTY CONVALESCENT HOSPITAL. He slaps the rag over the wound. I can't imagine a rag keeping back the flow of blood, but it does. Still, a dirty rag isn't something you use on an open wound.

"Mr. Jackson, maybe I should—"

"Get on home," he tells me. "Go on, your mother's home, I can hear her."

And he's right. My mother has just driven up.

"But. . . ." I don't know what to tell him. He holds the rag over his wound, the expression on his face unchanging, as if a tear in his arm is no more dangerous to him than a tear in his shirt. It looks as though the flow of blood has stopped, but to be honest, I never really saw a flow of blood begin.

I leave, thinking all kinds of troubled thoughts. As I head out of the yard I see, sitting on a cinder block, the waffles I brought him that morning, uneaten.

It's later that night. Mom's asleep on the sofa again, her book open in her lap. I dial the number it took me half an hour to track down and hear it ring once . . . twice . . . three times.

"Dade County Convalescent Hospital," answers a tired-sounding woman on the other end.

"I'm calling about a Mr. Isaac Jackson," I say.

A long pause on the other end, and then, "Are you a family member?"

"No. Listen, I think he's not quite right. I mean, he's here, and I think he's still supposed to be with you. I think he kind of . . . ran away."

"What do you mean he's there?" the woman says, sounding alarmed. "Who is this? Are you from the medical school?"

"I'm just a neighbor, that's all."

"It says right here that Isaac Jackson was transferred to the medical school last week."

I take the number of the medical school, and after we hang

up, I try that number. One ring . . . two rings. The guy who picks up the phone talks to me in between bites of his sandwich.

"Says here we were supposed to get him," he tells me. "But he never showed up. Probably just a clerical error."

By now I'm beginning to get upset. "Well, somebody should come and get him," I say. "I mean, what if he's in trouble?"

And on the other end I hear the creep laugh. "Ha! That's a good one!" he snorts. "No, he's not getting into any trouble anymore. Not unless those med students are playing practical jokes with their cadavers again."

My heart misses a hefty beat.

"Cadavers?"

"Yeah," says the guy as I hear him take another bite from his sandwich. "You know, as in *corpse*. As in *stiff*." He laughs again. "Yeah, those med students sure are clowns. Those things end up in the darndest places sometimes!"

I slam the phone down as if hanging up can somehow change what I've just heard. I don't believe it. And yet somehow I do. And somehow I understand.

Outside the clouds hide the moon, and it's as dark as if the moon weren't even there. As I step outside, it takes a few moments for my night vision to kick in. When it does, I find the hole in the wooden fence and cross over into the cold loneliness of Mr. Jackson's world.

I can hear him back there—hear him moaning. I can hear him working with his trowel. *Skitch . . . brummp, skitch . . . brummp* Slowly I round the corner where the drainpipe once stood, and there, in the center of the yard, is total darkness.

There isn't going to be a fountain there. That bald patch of dirt was not for a fountain at all. It was for a grave.

I peer into the hole, and see, at the bottom of a shallow hole,

Mr. Jackson covering himself with dirt. With one hand he weakly slices into the dirt wall and pulls it down around him.

"No time," he whispers to himself. "No time left. No time."

My eyes are full of tears, but I wipe them away.

"When did it happen, Mr. Jackson?" I ask him. And then I force out what I really mean to say. "When did you . . . die?"

He takes a deep breath, and it comes out like a raspy wheeze. "It'll be two weeks tomorrow," he says.

I swallow hard, choking down my own terror. "And you don't know where your family is, and no one would bury you?"

The only answer is that raspy wheeze.

I reach into the shallow hole and take the trowel away from Mr. Jackson. He begins to panic as I drag him out.

"No!" he says. "No time. No time. Getting too weak."

"Shhh!" I tell him gently. "Shhh. Someone will hear."

And then I look into those empty eyes that can barely stay open at all. I force myself to *keep* looking, this time refusing to look away from that awful face, trying to see the man he must have once been.

"What do you want me to do?" I ask.

In those ruined eyes I see tears beginning to form.

"Care for me," he says.

But I won't do that. Nurses and hospital workers care *for* him. But they can't care *about* him. Not the way I can.

I look at the grave. "It's not deep enough," I tell him. Then I grab the large shovel leaning up against the house, step into the hole, and begin digging, throwing dirt over my shoulder.

The old man tilts his head. I hear it creak and fracture on his slim neck. "You're a good boy, Jeremy," he says with a voice that keeps moving farther and farther back in his throat. "A good boy."

"Rest easy, Mr. Jackson. I'll give you a decent burial; you don't have to worry. I'll take care of everything, I promise . . ."

Mr. Jackson smiles his awful smile, but somehow that smile doesn't seem awful at all. It seems wonderful and warm and filled with the kind of peace that comes from knowing things are all right. That things are in order.

I watch as Mr. Jackson lets his shoulders relax, his eyes close, and his head sink to the ground, finally giving his spirit over to the death that had been trying to claim his body. In a moment I know that he is gone—*truly* gone, the way he should have been two weeks ago.

Now I'm alone, as I stand here in the darkness of his backyard garden, digging his grave.

I will bury you, Mr. Jackson. I will bury you in the place where you lived your good years. I will cover your grave with flowers, so it will be our secret, and you can rest, knowing that there was someone in this world willing to see you off into the next.

And I will not be afraid.

Skitch . . . brummp.

Skitch . . . Brummp.

CALEB'S COLORS

···

A dark hat. A dark coat. A tall figure standing in the doorway, silhouetted by the stark streetlight.

"My name is Quentin Prax. I'm here about your son."

I didn't like him. Not at first. The way he spoke, it was so slow, so practiced and smooth. The way he said his name— hissing it like a snake. *Praxsssssss.*

"We've been expecting you," said my father.

The man stepped into the light of the living room, where I could see that his dark coat was not black but brown. Not just brown though—it was woven of many different colors, all intertwined until they blended perfectly into a rich mahogany. His eyes locked on mine, and he smiled. I had to look away. His smile was unnerving. It could not be read. Like his coat, it seemed to be woven of so many different thoughts and meanings that I didn't know what that smile was for.

"You must be the sister," he said to me through that smile.

I didn't like being called "the sister." "My name's Rhia," I told him. He smiled again.

"Rhia. What a colorful name."

He strolled across our living room as if he were welcome, and my parents didn't do anything about it. His presence was so powerful, my parents had no response.

Prax turned to Caleb, my little brother. Caleb sat at the kitchen table, the place he could most often be found, with a box of Crayolas. His left hand moved across a piece of paper, leaving periwinkle streaks.

When you first watch Caleb and his Crayolas, you might think his marks are random—just wild firings from a ruined brain—but watch long enough, and you'll see shapes forming out of those wild lines, until you suddenly realize that you're looking at a sailing ship, or a mountain range, or a lion that seems so real you'd swear it might leap off the page at you.

And Caleb does all this without even looking at the page. He'll just sit there, staring forward, rocking back and forth, in a way that could make you seasick just watching him.

"This must be Caleb," said Mr. Prax. "How are you, Caleb?"

"He won't answer you," I told the man. "He doesn't talk."

But Mr. Prax only smiled that many-colored smile once more and said, "Oh, he does. He just doesn't care to use words." I tried to stare this Mr. Prax down, but I couldn't. People who came to help Caleb promised us the moon, then they took our money and left Caleb no better than they found him. Caleb's condition gave my parents enough to fight about without having to argue over quack doctors—which is exactly what

I figured Prax was. He smiled at me again, then he turned to my parents. "May we talk in private?"

"Rhia," said my mother, "why don't you take Caleb upstairs and get him ready for bed."

I was irritated that I couldn't be a part of whatever was going on, but also relieved that I could be out of Mr. Prax's sight. I didn't trust him. He seemed far too calculating and mysterious. I didn't like mysteries—especially when they were strutting around my house.

I took Caleb's hand and lifted him to his feet. He followed me upstairs quietly tonight. Sometimes it's not so easy. Sometimes he would whine and pull his hair. Sometimes he would scream like the end of the world had come. I had grown used to all of that—I had had to, because putting him to bed was a responsibility I had chosen to take on. But tonight he didn't kick and scream; he merely followed.

I took him to his room and dressed him for bed. All the time he stared forward with that blank, nonseeing look of his. He could stare for hours at the TV like that, and I always wondered what he saw there. Light and colors? Shapes moving back and forth? There were times when he would take a crayon to paper and recreate, line for line, the image of something he had seen on TV, as if his mind was a VCR, recording everything it saw. Then there would be the times he would draw things too strange and exotic to have come from anywhere in this world. In one moment he would draw a place of terror so dark I could not bear to look at it, and then in the next instant turn the page over and draw a world of such intense beauty it would make me truly know that there was a God somewhere, because who else could put such a beautiful image into the head of a small, autistic boy?

That was life with Caleb. A never-ending gallery of Crayola wonders that papered the wall of his room, floor to ceiling. Me, I could barely draw a stick figure . . . but it didn't make me jealous. How could I be jealous of a brother whose whole world had no room for anything but himself and his Crayolas?

I finished dressing Caleb for bed and left him. Sneaking out onto the stairs, I peeked down into the kitchen, where Mr. Prax sat with my parents.

"I've done much work with idiot savants," said Mr. Prax. I bristled at the expression "idiot savant." That's the label the world gives people like Caleb. People whose brain somehow got wired to do one thing and one thing only. There were people who could do instant math like a super-computer but had to be taught to feed themselves. There were some who could memorize hundreds of books just by skimming through them but couldn't hold a conversation. I'd even heard of a little girl labeled as severely retarded who designed an aircraft for the military.

Dad sat with his arms crossed. Mom had called Prax on the advice of a friend, but it had been a long time since Dad trusted therapists.

"Caleb's had every therapy in the book," said Dad. "I doubt yours will help any more than the others did."

"You don't understand," said Mr. Quentin Prax sharply. "I'm not here as a therapist, I'm here as an employer. I'm the owner of a small but prestigious art gallery specializing in unique works of art. Perhaps you've heard of it: the Galleria du Mondes."

My parents seemed as surprised as I was. If he wasn't a doctor, then what did he want with Caleb?

"We don't know of it," admitted my mother. "We're not really art patrons . . ."

"My gallery seeks out . . . special artists with unique talents," Prax told them. "A colleague of mine came across one of Caleb's sketches and sent it to me. I was quite impressed."

Mom stiffened in her chair. Until now she had watched Prax with wide and hopeful eyes. But now it seemed her hope was draining fast.

"Just what is it you want, Mr. Prax?" she said coldly.

Prax grinned at her. "Simple," he said. "I would like to commission a large work from him."

Mom laughed, and Dad, well, he just got angry.

"Listen," said my father. "We've got a little boy with a lot of problems. I don't like the idea of hiring him out as some sort of creative freak for the amusement of a bunch of snobs."

Mr. Prax looked down at his perfectly manicured fingernails, unconcerned with my father's anger. "You misunderstand," he said. "The sole purpose of my gallery is to give expression to creativity that would otherwise be lost. Your son has a gift, and I'd like to help him share it with the world." Mr. Prax paused for a moment, then took a deep breath and said, "I have a special interest, you see, because my own daughter was very much like your boy."

"Was?" questioned Mom.

"She's no longer with me."

"I'm sorry," said Mom.

My father sighed, on the verge of giving in. "How much will this cost?" he asked.

Mr. Prax laughed heartily at that—loud enough that it made me jump. "It won't cost you, my friend, it will only cost me," he said. Then he pulled an envelope out of his pocket and handed it to my father, who opened it and began laughing. There was a check in the envelope.

"All right, who put you up to this?" he chuckled. "Was it Joe at work? He's always pulling practical jokes."

"No joke," said Prax, completely serious. "And that's

only half. The other half is payable on completion of the work."

My mother was gasping as if she were hyperventilating.

"A million dollars? For a drawing by Caleb?"

"My gallery has some very wealthy patrons."

I could hardly believe it myself. I thought of the way Mom and Dad always bought those stupid lottery tickets, even though a person's more likely to get struck by lightning five times than to win once—and now the jackpot comes walking right into our living room.

"I'm sure Caleb's condition has left you with a great many medical expenses," reminded Prax. "This will pay those expenses with more than enough left over for you."

Well, Caleb might not talk, but money does, and Mr. Prax had himself a deal. As they came walking out of the kitchen, I tried to scoot up the stairs, into the shadows, where I couldn't be seen—but Prax saw me nonetheless. He stared at me with that strange smile again.

"Rhia," said Mr. Prax. "I would very much like you to come to my gallery and assist your brother in his creation."

I shrunk back even further.

"I don't do what he does," I told him.

"Of course not," said Prax. "But every artist needs an assistant."

"No," I told him. I wouldn't be bought, like my parents were.

My parents turned to me in shock, as if I had just thrown a stone through a plate glass window, then my mother turned back to Mr. Prax.

"Rhia will be happy to go," declared my mother. Then she turned to me. "After all, it's summer vacation, so she has plenty of time, don't you, Rhia?"

I didn't trust this Mr. Prax, no matter how much money he

had. He wasn't just a rich guy who liked to help autistic kids—there was much more to him than that. Still, this was a battle I knew I couldn't win. Three adults and a million dollars against little ol' me. No matter how far I wanted to be away from Prax, I knew I was destined to spend days, maybe weeks, with the eerie man, watching Caleb paint.

"Fine," I said. "I'll go, but only because I want to make sure Caleb's treated right."

"Splendid," said Prax. "I'd like Caleb and Rhia at my gallery at nine o'clock sharp tomorrow morning."

After Mr. Prax had gone, I went back up to Caleb's room, where he sat on the edge of his bed, exactly where I'd left him.

I stretched him out and pulled the covers over him. He lay there looking up at the ceiling—a ceiling that was covered with his Crayola creations.

"Do you know you're worth a million dollars, Caleb," I said to him. He blinked, but showed no signs of hearing me. "Do you even know what a million dollars is?" Still no response. I don't know why I always expected him to say something.

"Good night, Caleb. I love you." I turned off the light, went to my room, and slipped into a sleep filled with nightmares I couldn't remember.

Caleb and I took a bus to Mr. Prax's gallery, but instead of bringing us inside, he took us for a ride in his white Mercedes limousine. The limousine, he told us, was a gift from one of the clients of his gallery. I wondered how anyone—even a rich person—could give away a limousine.

We drove for an hour, into the heart of the city, until we stopped at an immense museum of art. All afternoon we wandered through the maze of exhibits.

"See how Manet uses light to capture the moment of sunset here," Prax said at one point. "See how Van Gogh's thick textures bring the night sky to life," he said at another. "See how the tiny points of color in Seurat's work blend together the farther away you stand." Gallery after gallery, he had something to say about every artist, every painting, until my mind was so full of color and texture that all I could see was gray.

"Why are you doing this?" I finally asked him. "Caleb doesn't care. He's not listening to you. He doesn't know a Monet from a Manet from a Schmanet. He's retarded," I hated the word, but I was angry. "He's worse than retarded. Don't you understand that?"

Then he looked at me with that same cold stare he gave my father the night before. "I'm not talking to him. I'm talking to *you*."

"Me?"

I looked at Caleb, whose eyes wandered around, giving as much time to the thermostat on the wall as they did to the paintings.

"Caleb needs no words to tell him about these paintings," said Mr. Prax.

"So why are you telling me about it?" I asked.

"So that maybe you'll be able to understand some of the things he already knows," was Prax's answer. Then he asked me something I'll never forget.

"Do you think that these artists were masters?"

"Sure," I said. "I guess."

Prax shook his head. "No. These artists could only bring a hint of greatness to their canvases. Shadows of possibilities, nothing more. They are failures." And then he leaned in close to me. "Would you like to see the work of real masters?"

And although I didn't want to go anywhere else with Mr.

Prax today, curiosity had already begun to drill deep into my brain. I nodded my head and said, "Yes. Yes I do."

He took us back to his gallery, where the walls were covered with canvases filled with dripping splotches of brown paint.

"You call these masterpieces?" I asked. "Looks like a lot of mud to me."

He shook his head. "This isn't the gallery. The real gallery is upstairs."

He opened a door and took us up a narrow staircase into a huge loft. It must have once been a factory or something, because it had brick walls, and lots of windows—but those windows were all painted over.

Surrounding us were dozens upon dozens of sheet-covered canvases, all five- or six-feet tall, and all resting upon heavy wooden easels. In the dim light of the huge loft, they looked like ghosts all facing in different directions.

He locked the door behind us.

"These are the works of the masters," he said and began to pull away the sheets that covered them one by one.

Any doubts I had were gone the moment I laid eyes on that first canvas.

It was a landscape like nothing I had ever seen, and trying to explain it now is like trying to explain sight to a blind person. These were colors the human eye had never before seen. Colors that had no names, depicting a place too strange and surreal to be of this world.

The second masterpiece was in a different set of hues, but just as incredible: A scene of clouds billowing upward toward a sun that actually shone, lighting up the room. Deep within the painting, golden winged beings seemed caught in a glorious journey toward that sun.

The third was the most magnificent of all. A forest of impossibly exotic trees, swirling in a greenish mist. Hills rolled into the distance, and in the foreground the single limb of a tree curved downward, with a smattering of red leaves. It seemed so real I could almost smell the rich fragrances of the forest and feel the slow breeze that made the mist swim and shimmer. It was unearthly, and otherworldly, like the other paintings.

"You wish to touch the painting," said Prax. It wasn't so much a question as a statement of fact. "You may do so. These paintings are meant to be touched."

I reached out toward one of those redder-than-red leaves to feel its velvet texture . . .

. . . and when I drew my hand away, I was holding the leaf between my fingers!

I gasped, and let the leaf flutter to the ground.

Prax smiled. "The task of the artist," he said, "is the creation of worlds. Very few succeed. Many die trying."

In a small room behind the great gallery was a paint-splattered studio, and in that studio were a palette, brushes, and about a thousand brand-new tubes of paint. All set up in front of a canvas the same size as the others in the gallery. Only this canvas was empty.

Caleb stood just a few inches away from the canvas, staring that blank stare of his, and Mr. Prax put a paintbrush in Caleb's hand.

"Do you believe in miracles, Rhia?"

To be honest, I didn't know. But then my brother began to paint. Thick, heavy brush strokes. In moments Caleb had begun creating a bright, wonderful work of art.

Then I saw something out of the corner of my eye. There was something shiny in Prax's hand. Shiny and sharp. I gasped and pulled Caleb away from the canvas as Prax brought the carving knife down ... slashing through the center of the canvas. The fabric shredded from top to bottom.

"No!" he screamed furiously at Caleb. "Look at those brush strokes! This is Van Gogh!" I was so shocked, all I could do was push myself back against the wall in disbelief.

Caleb screamed as if he himself had been stabbed and didn't stop screaming until Prax brought another canvas. He quieted immediately and silently resumed painting. He dabbed his brush against the canvas lightly, creating tiny little points of light. Again Prax's knife came down, shredding the emerging work.

"No!" Prax yelled. "This is Seurat."

Caleb wailed again and began to rock feverishly back and forth. Once more Prax brought a fresh canvas.

I wanted to grab Caleb and run, taking him away from this ranting, insane man—and yet part of me must have understood what he was doing, and why he was doing it. Because I stayed. I stayed to witness Caleb's terrifying ordeal.

"We're not leaving here," shouted Prax, "until we're done. Even if it takes days. Weeks. Months."

On and on it went. I began crying, begging Prax to stop, but he wouldn't. He shredded canvas after canvas—one that looked like a Manet, and another like a Picasso. Caleb barely had a chance to get down a single brush stroke before that awful knife would come down again, sending him into a screaming fit, each one worse than the one before.

And then Caleb just shut down.

Prax put a new canvas in front of him, and Caleb didn't move. He stood there, red in the face, staring at the white fabric with an expression of emptiness worse than ever before—

as if he were staring through the canvas with no emotion. No mind. He didn't even try to paint.

"Now you've done it!" I shouted at Prax through my tears. "Now he'll never paint or pick up a crayon ever again! You've ruined the one thing he can do, you monster."

Prax didn't answer me; he just looked at Caleb, waiting. Then I heard the faraway jingling of bells, and Prax left to greet a customer who had just arrived downstairs. He closed the door behind him, and Caleb and I were alone with the horribly empty canvas.

"Caleb," I whispered. "Caleb, you don't have to paint. You don't have to do anything. We'll get you home. I'll tuck you in bed. It'll be just like it always was. You'd like that, wouldn't you?"

Nothing. Caleb didn't even rock back and forth. Something was very, very wrong, and I cursed Prax for doing this to him.

That's when I heard voices outside the door. I peeked through the keyhole to see Prax—his slick, smooth self leading a couple through the great secret gallery. The man and woman hardly looked rich enough to invest in great works of art. In fact, they looked poor, worn, and tired, as if they'd seen more trouble and pain than most.

The man knelt down on the gallery floor, opened up a suitcase, and showed its contents to Prax.

"It's all there," said the man wearily. "Every penny we could find. Everything we own."

"I'm afraid it's not very much," the woman apologized.

Prax waved the remark away. I guess he didn't care how much it was. "Have you chosen a work that suits you?" he asked.

The man and woman stepped toward the surreal landscape with the red leaves.

"Ah," said Prax, smiling his multicolored smile for them. "My daughter's. I hope you enjoy it."

And with that I could see the look of world-weariness leave the couple's faces. How would they carry it out, I wondered—it was such a huge canvas.

I leaned back to brush some hair from my face, and when I peeked through the hole again, the couple was gone . . .

. . . and a single leaf, redder than red, fluttered to the floor at Prax's feet. My heart missed a very long beat.

Prax immediately covered the painting with a sheet, and turned.

"Come out, Rhia," he said, knowing I was there all along. "The door isn't locked."

I stepped into the gallery and helped Mr. Prax adjust the sheet on the painting so it hung just right.

Prax seemed to sigh in satisfaction, then closed the suitcase. I noticed it only seemed to have a few crumpled bills.

"This world we live in," said Prax, "is kind to some, but cruel to others. For those who would rather not be here, I provide . . . alternatives." Then he smiled at me, and although his smile still seemed filled with many strange colors, I felt I could understand some of them now. "Perhaps there will come a time," he said, "when everyone will have to choose a masterpiece."

The smell of oil paint seemed to grow stronger around me, and I turned to see that Caleb had begun painting. He was working feverishly—and this time it was different from before. As I stepped back into the studio, I could see the speed at which his fingers were moving. They were a blur. Even the colors he was putting on that canvas seemed far brighter, far more special than the colors that came from the tubes of paint.

All the time he stared through that white canvas as if the

work was already there behind it and he wasn't so much brushing on paint as he was brushing away the emptiness. Soon he threw the paintbrush away and began to use his fingers, spreading and blending the colors from corner to corner. For half an hour we watched in awed silence, and half an hour was all it took.

"My God!" I said when it was done, but my words seemed far away, lost in the depth of the painting.

It was something entirely new, nothing like what any artist anywhere had ever created. The world Caleb had made was both wilderness and city, both earth and sky. Wild winds swept through magnificent trees toward gleaming crystalline spires. Brilliant shafts of light spilled upon peaceful hills, and yet the light was balanced by deep shafts of darkness that swam with unknowable mysteries. Still, as new as all this was, it was somehow familiar. It was then that I realized that everything in this great work I'd seen before. A fragment on the refrigerator door. A sketch on Caleb's wall. Everything Caleb had ever drawn was just a shadow of this, his great work. His one work.

I reached toward it, wanting more than anything to reach into it—and instead I got my fingers covered with paint.

Caleb smoothed over the smudge I had made with my fingers.

"It's not finished," said Mr. Prax. "It needs a signature."

"But Caleb can't write his name."

Mr. Prax shook his head. "That's not the kind of signature I mean." Then Prax leaned over and whispered into Caleb's ear. "Go on, Caleb. Finish it."

And with that, Caleb reached forward and pressed his spread fingers against the center of his creation. He grit his teeth. He squinted his eyes and pushed that hand against the canvas with all his soul, until finally his hand punched through . . . into a world rich with colors. I could see the canvas changing, the flatness of it stretching out and back like a wave was rolling through it, until its depth reached the infinite horizon.

Caleb looked at his fingers there inside of his painting, watching the light playing off of them . . . then he lurched forward and leapt into it. Once inside, he threw his hands out. He spun around. He was dancing—Caleb was actually dancing! And then for the first time in his life he turned his head to look at me. And he smiled. It was a smile filled with more colors than Mr. Prax's. That's when I knew Caleb was finally where he belonged. Caleb didn't waste time saying good-bye. He turned and ran, hopped and skipped deep into his world, until he disappeared in a place the canvas did not show.

My joy to have seen him so happy overwhelmed my grief at knowing he was gone. With my eyes full of tears, I reached my hand into that world too. I felt the warmth of that strange light. How I wanted to launch myself in there as well, but Mr. Prax had something else in mind.

"I need a gatekeeper," he told me. "Someone to decide whom Caleb would want in his world. Will you do that for me?"

I didn't answer him. Instead I went to a shelf, opened a sheet, and together we gently covered the canvas.

That night we brought Mom and Dad to the gallery, to show them the masterpiece—and although my parents can be thick as a brick sometimes, one look at the painting and they understood. My mother cried tears of both joy and loss, as I had. My father hid his feelings by comforting her.

Since then, I've been taking my own art lessons. I still don't know much about art, but I do know that there are places inside of us—palaces of glorious light and caverns of unknowable darkness. Magical places filled with brilliant, unimaginable colors that we suffer to bring forth.

I know I could never suffer the way Caleb did—to imagine a place so perfectly that it becomes real—but if someday I can paint just a shadow of the possibilities . . . perhaps that will be enough.

RALPHY SHERMAN'S JACUZZI OF WONDERS

••

We were sitting in our hot tub, minding our own business, when *she* came out to join us. Vermelda.

Roxanne, my younger sister, let out a groan. "Ugh! Here it comes," said Roxanne. "Do you think it will want to sit in here with us?"

"Pretend we don't see her, maybe she'll go away," I said, but unfortunately Vermelda did have a mind of her own—amazingly small though it was—and she was determined to warm up to us and force us to like her. She was my father's girlfriend, you see, but we knew she was after his money, just like all the others. Needless to say, we didn't like her very much.

"Hi Ralphy, hi Roxanne," she said with a pretty capped-toothed smile. "Can I join you?" Her skimpy polka-dot bikini made her look like she'd walked right out of a Coppertone ad.

"I guess," I told her. "It's a free country."

She dipped a pink-painted toe into the water. "Ooh, it's hot," she said.

"The better to boil you with," responded Roxanne.

Vermelda chuckled uncomfortably, slipped her foot in inch by inch, and descended into the bubbling tub of chlorinated water. She sat next to us and tried to make conversation.

"We were talking about foreign languages," I told her, "and how funny some words are."

"Really," she said.

"Yes," I told her. "For instance, in Mexico, the most popular brand of bread is called *Bimbo*."

Roxanne nodded. "Bimbo bread," she said. "Only in Mexico, they pronounce it like this: *Beeembo!*"

I looked at Vermelda and smiled widely. *"Beeeeeeembo,"* I said, very slowly.

"Well, that's certainly interesting," said Vermelda, lowering her shoulders into the water. "So," she said, "your father's told me a lot about both of you."

I kicked my feet just enough to get her hair wet. "Really," I said. "He hasn't told us anything about you."

"But," added Roxanne, "I think we know everything we need to know."

Vermelda smiled uncertainly.

"Be careful where you sit," I told her. "People have been known to disappear in this Jacuzzi before."

"Disappear," repeated Vermelda. "What do you mean 'disappear'?"

I raised my eyebrows. "Exactly what you think, Miss Hyde: They come, they have a soak, and they're never heard from again."

"Yes," chimed in Roxanne, "it's a mystery never fully explained."

Vermelda wagged a press-on nail at us. "You two!" she said. "Your father told me about you and your stories." But the way we just smiled when she said that made her even more uncomfortable. So she changed the subject.

She looked up at the trees, then down the long expanse of our sizable backyard. "It must be nice," she said, "to live in such a big house. Your father must get lonely with no one to share it with. No one grown-up, I mean." And then she added, "I'm so sorry about your mother. It must have been terrible for you to have her taken from you so young."

"Oh," sighed Roxanne, "she'll be back."

Vermelda looked at us with the clueless eyes of a lab rat. "But . . . but I thought . . ."

"Yes, that's what everyone thinks," said Roxanne.

"But the truth is," I told her, "she was abducted by aliens."

"Oh really," said Vermelda, clearly not believing a word of our testimony.

"Mm-hmm," I said. "Right here in this very backyard. The ship came out of the trees and sucked her up through a straw."

"Pretty amazing," added Roxanne. "I saw it through my window. It's one of my earliest childhood memories."

"We get postcards from her occasionally," I said.

"But we can't read them," finished Roxanne. "On account of they're written in Alien."

A pulse of water surged in the Jacuzzi. A big bubble surfaced. It was getting dark, and the lights in the hot tub made it look like a bubbling vat of radioactive acid.

Suddenly, Roxanne sat up straight.

"I think it's down there," she whispered. "I felt it brush past my toes."

"Felt what?" asked Vermelda, pulling in her knees.

"You know," I said with a friendly grin. "The Loch Ness Monster."

Vermelda sighed, relaxed, and crossed her arms. "Now come on, Ralphy," she scolded. "I mean, some of the stories I've heard you tell are good—really good—but the Loch Ness Monster? In a Jacuzzi? How could that be possible?"

Roxanne looked at her with scientific seriousness. "We think there might be a space-time worm-hole."

"This Jacuzzi's much deeper than it looks," I explained. "It's so murky—Dad never cleans it out. You can't even see the bottom, can you?"

"No," said Vermelda. "But . . ."

I lowered myself into the water until my lips were just above the surface. "I sent my toy submarine down there once, with a camera attached," I said. "It went down, but it never came back."

The water continued to churn. The pump sounded like the engine of a great ship, a submerged groan, deep and hollow. I grinned.

"You know," announced Vermelda, her face getting more twisted and furious-looking by the minute, "a good boarding school would help the two of you learn the difference between fact and fiction. Someone ought to persuade your father to send you to one."

Roxanne folded her arms and stuck her nose in the air. "If you don't believe us, ask Dad."

"Of course, Dad probably won't tell you," I added. "He's trained to conceal the truth, no matter how much he's tortured."

Vermelda looked at us sideways. "Excuse me?"

"You know. They teach you that stuff when you're a spy," Roxanne whispered.

I rapped my sister on the arm. "Roxanne, we're not supposed to tell!"

"Oh yeah, I forgot."

"Your father's an accountant," insisted Vermelda. "I met him when he was doing my taxes."

"A *cover*," I explained. "I mean, do you really think an accountant could afford a house like this?"

Vermelda looked at us like a snooty poodle. "Maybe he got the money from the aliens," she said, painting on the sarcasm as thickly as she applied her mascara. "And they pay to keep him quiet about your mother's abduction."

My sister's lips quivered and I could see her pushing the tears out of her eyes. "You think that's funny?" shouted Roxanne, through the tears. "You think it's fun to tease small children who have no mother?"

Vermelda took on that laboratory rat look again. "But . . . but I was just playing the game—you know? Playing along with you two."

I took Roxanne under my arm and shot Vermelda an accusing glance. "You really don't have to be so cruel. Making fun of us. Calling our lives just a game."

"And I thought you were nice," pouted Roxanne.

I stared across the surface of the pool. The currents of the churning water seemed to change slightly.

"Ooh!" said Roxanne suddenly. "There it goes again. Did you feel it?"

"That," proclaimed Vermelda, "was not the Loch Ness Monster. It was your foot."

I shrugged. "Maybe it was, and maybe it wasn't."

Vermelda shivered.

"Cold?" Roxanne asked.

Actually, the water around our toes *was* beginning to feel a bit chilly.

"Hmmm," I said. "It's as if water is being pumped in from a different source."

"There!" shouted Roxanne. "Don't you see it?" She was pointing to the center of the huge tub.

Vermelda jumped in spite of herself. Her knees were locked up tight against her ample chest, and she was staring wide eyed at the bubbles. It's amazing the things you can see in the shifting shapes of hot tub bubbles. I don't know what she saw, but she did start to look just a little bit anxious.

"Oh!" growled Vermelda, furious. "Now you listen here, you little mucus-nosed brats! There's nothing in here but you and me. The bottom is only four feet deep, and I'll prove it by standing up!"

"I wouldn't do that if I were you," I warned.

"Shut up, you!" she barked.

She stood up. She went down.

I shrugged. "I tried to tell her," I said to Roxanne as we both gazed into the bubbling water. Then with a *blub-sputter-cough!* up came Vermelda, her perfectly coiffed hair now a wet mess hanging over her face.

"Help me!" she gurgled, reaching out her hand.

Roxanne and I just looked on with pity. "Can't you swim?" asked Roxanne.

And that's when *it* appeared.

Suddenly, from the center of the Jacuzzi, the creature's immense head rose up from the water and grabbed Vermelda in its wide, tooth-filled mouth.

Vermelda tried to scream, but the thing swallowed her in a single gulp. We watched a bulge slip down the creature's long neck, like a snake swallowing a mouse.

The monster roared, then pulled its head back down through the Jacuzzi, squeezing way, way down to the bottomless depths, where, in some way that we don't quite understand, our Jacuzzi connected to that famous Scottish lake.

Of course the monster never came after us. After all, we fed it.

The tub returned to normal, except for the fact that it wasn't hot anymore. Now the only sound was the endless churning of the murky water. A single press-on nail came floating on the current of lukewarm bubbles and bumped against the side.

Roxanne shook her head. "Some people just don't listen," she said and reached over to turn up the heat.

Dad came out into the backyard a few minutes later, wondering where Vermelda had gone.

"Nessie ate her," we told him.

He shook his head sadly. "Not again. Didn't you warn her?"

"Of course we did," I told him. "But she had a mind of her own."

"How awful," said Dad. "Who's going to eat that extra steak tonight?"

"You can take it with you," I suggested, "and eat it on your way to the Pentagon tomorrow."

Dad sighed in resignation and turned off the Jacuzzi. The light went out and the bubbles settled. "All right, come on inside, you two. There's a postcard from Mom in the kitchen."

"Really?" Roxanne raced off into the house, still dripping wet, and I followed.

Of course we couldn't read the card, but man, the picture on the front was great!

NUMBER TWO

....

A *purpose,* he thinks, *a purpose in life. Everyone has a purpose in life.* Yes, this is true—it has to be true—but what is his purpose? Will he have to search it out in a long quest, or will it come to him on wings, in a vision or a dream? Someone with great wisdom has brought him into this world—would that someone ever tell him why?

And how long would he have to wait for an answer?

Not long.

Not long at all.

Pulled out of darkness, and into a bright light he has never known before. Shapes swirl all around him, moving colors and lights, all out of focus. An eye, a face, a soft, warm hand lifting him up, making him feel wanted, needed. He wants to cry out with joy, if he only knew how to cry. Sounds of voices, talking, laughing.

And a grinding noise.

Moving now. Moving across the room, through the light, and toward the noise.

"Wait your turn," a voice says sternly.

In the center of the light is a round shape, and in the center of that round shape is a dark hole.

Moving out of the light and into darkness again, into the dark hole, filled with a strong, musty odor. His head is firmly caught in the darkness.

Tight.

Uncomfortable.

He begins to panic.

And the grinding noise starts once again. Loud, all around him—around his head, grinding and slicing.

Spinning blades.

Sharp gnashing gears, grinding against each other—they slice deep into him, cutting away. He screams, but no one can hear over the grinding. *Help me! Help me, please! Something's gone wrong!*

If someone listens, someone has to hear.

I'm alive.

If someone knows, someone has to care.

But the slicing, gnashing knives carve deep, taking pieces of him away forever. Cruel. Unfeeling.

Until all that is left of his head is a dark pinpoint. His soft sensitive core, once protected, is now exposed to the world.

Out of the darkness, into the light again, moving through the air that painfully blows across the pale open wound.

The soft hand that had given him so much warmth before now holds him too tightly and flips him upside down. His aching face is pressed against a rough, flat surface and scraped against it, like a nose to the grindstone, until bits of him are left behind, silver-gray traces of his life draining away onto the clean coarse surface.

This can't be it! This can't be my purpose! he screams. *I am meant for more! Much, much more! Doesn't anyone hear me?*

But all that can be heard of his screaming is a gentle *hisssssss* as the little girl presses his face to the rough page and writes:

How I spent my summer vacation

THE SOUL EXCHANGE

....

Down the long, empty corridor, in the chrome and tile bathroom of Bloomingdale's, Nina closely examines a zit in the mirror.

Her face, in every other way, is perfect, but that's not what Nina sees. She sees the ugly whitehead on her cheek and thinks it's Vesuvius about to erupt and wipe out Pompeii. She imagines half of Manhattan must know about the zit by now. Her stunning green eyes, her shimmering red hair, mean nothing to her as long as that *thing* sits on her face.

"I hate myself," she mumbles. "I'm sooo ugly!"

The lonely restroom is not so lonely. An old woman has entered. She comes to the mirror beside Nina and tries, with bony, shaking hands, to put lipstick on her thin lips. Nina notices how the crone's rouge sits on her wrinkled cheekbones, round and far too red. She looks like a clown. Nina has no love, nor patience, for the elderly. To her, a woman like this has no business wearing makeup. What good is it going to do? You'd need a cement mixer to hold the makeup it would take to spackle in those wrinkles. You'd need a machete to cut through the hairy mole on her chin.

The old woman steals a sideways glance at Nina in the mirror. Her eyes are narrow, and cloudy.

"What are *you* looking at?" says Nina. Her voice booms far too loud around the gray-tiled room.

"You have a pimple," says the woman, her voice as rough as sandpaper. Probably from smoking, thinks Nina. Stupid woman. It's a miracle she's even lived this long.

"I know about the pimple," says Nina, striking an irritated pose. "So why don't you mind your own business."

Nina dots the solitary spot with Clearasil. Still the old woman looks at her sideways. The woman, Nina notes, wears an ill-fitting coat that must have been very expensive once. Some sort of fur. But now it's moth-eaten, and mangy. She wears jewelry also—not the cheap imitation stuff, but the real thing. A diamond as big as an almond. What a waste for something so precious to be on someone so wretched, thinks Nina.

"I couldn't help but hear you, dear," says the old woman. "You sound very, very unhappy with yourself. You poor thing."

Nina looks at herself in the mirror again and grimaces at her own reflection. It's not right. It's not perfect enough. She wants to rip her awful face off and flush it down the drain. Her best friend, Heather McKnee, is prettier. She hates, hates, hates Heather McKnee, but most of all she hates her own face, and the zit it gave birth to.

The old woman smiles, and her thin lips disappear, revealing two rows of yellow teeth. "I understand what you're going through," the old woman says.

"How can *you* understand anything?" snaps Nina.

"My bones may be old," says the woman, "but my mind is still keen. I remember my youth." Then she reaches into her pocket and pulls out a business card, holding it out to Nina with a quivering hand.

"Give him a call," she says. "He's sure to help. He knows what you need."

Then the old woman turns and limps toward the door. Nina follows her out and watches as, cane in hand, the woman makes the long trek down the empty hallway to the department store.

Nina looks at the card. Burgundy lettering on a shiny gray background.

Dr. Morgan Taylor Voyd
Discorporeal Physician
Extractions and implants while-u-wait

Nina, not being blessed with vocabulary skills, has no clue what any of it means, but the chicken salad in her stomach doesn't feel too happy about it. Suddenly, Nina doesn't feel like shopping today.

Tonight is pizza night for the "in" group at East End Private Academy. On pizza night, they go out to Little Guido's and eat pepperoni pies with extra cheese, then talk about all the people they hate, such as teachers, parents, and anyone who's not at the table with them.

Heather McKnee is there, and as she arrives Nina says a silent die-slowly-and-painfully prayer to herself, about Heather; then they sit to eat. Nina sits next to Brent, her boyfriend of the month. But she'd much rather be sitting next to Heather's boyfriend. He's a ninth-grader, and goalie of the junior varsity soccer team. Brent, on the other hand, is in eighth grade like the rest of them. He's captain of the eighth-grade wrestling team. Big deal.

Brent sits there, with his arm clamped around her shoulder, like they were Siamese twins, connected at the wrist and neck.

"I'll just have a salad," says Heather. "I don't need all that grease." And then she looks at Nina and adds, "It could give me zits."

Nina smiles, pretending that it doesn't bother her. She can feel the zit on her face, like a big, fat pepperoni. She turns her face away so that the others can't see it, but they do. Her friends have radar when it comes to how a person looks. They can spot an out-of-place hair from a hundred yards. They can smell a dying fashion trend like body odor.

Brent looks at Nina's face, as if she had pulled off a mask to reveal she was the Phantom of the Opera. He takes his hand from her shoulder, releasing her from his boyfriendly head-lock. "You know," he says, "there's soaps you could use for that."

"Ha, ha," says Nina, covering it with her hand and intensifying her silent death-prayer toward Heather. When the pizza comes, Nina refuses to eat. Instead she pulls out the card the old woman gave her. Dr. Morgan Taylor Voyd.

"Who's he?" asks Brent, looking over her shoulder.

"Some doctor," says Nina. She tries to hide the card, but Brent pulls it away. He looks at it, but it might as well be written in Chinese.

"What is he, a zit doctor?" asks Brent.

"No, he's a discorporeal physician," she says, trying to sound wise, as if she knows what it means.

Brent passes the card around the table to Nina's humiliation.

"Must be a shrink," says Heather. "A good therapist can really help with emotional problems."

"He's not that kind of doctor!" insists Nina. "And anyway, I'm not going to see him." She grabs the card back, crumples it up, and hurls it across the room. It lands right in the trash.

"Two points!" announces Brent and slips her into his boyfriendly headlock again, in spite of the zit.

Brent talks about himself as he walks Nina home. How annoying. Nina much prefers the boyfriends that will talk about her. Brent is in the middle of professing his undying belief that there's nothing fake about professional wrestling when Nina interrupts him.

"Brent, do you think I'm pretty?" she asks.

Brent shrugs. "Yeah, sure, why not?" he says—which doesn't mean much, because Brent would say anything as long as he got to show her off to his friends in public places.

"Am I prettier than Heather?" Nina dares to ask.

Brent hesitates. "Well ..." he says, "you're both pretty. You're just pretty in different ways."

The answer infuriates Nina. She takes his hand and pulls it behind his back in a move that rivals the best of wrestlers.

"Ow!" yells Brent. "Lemme go! What's the deal?"

"You were supposed to say 'yes,' " she tells him. She pushes him away and heads off in the other direction. Brent, still dumbfounded, doesn't follow.

She retraces her steps down First Avenue and ducks back into Little Guido's. Then she digs through the trash, past greasy half-eaten slices of pizza and sticky soft-drink residue, until she finds the crumpled business card.

Deep in the unknowable parts of Brooklyn, overgrown sycamores line the streets of the old neighborhood where the doctor lives. Their roots buckle the sidewalk into concrete accordion folds. The homes are brown brick, and although it's a bright day, the trees block out every trace of the sun.

Halfway down the street, a shingle hangs outside the doctor's home office. M. T. VOYD, reads the shingle. *Appointments required.* Nina has already made her appointment.

She rings the bell, and a moment later the doctor answers the door.

"Come in, Nina, I've been waitin' for you," he says with a heavy Jamaican accent. He is a tall man, as gaunt as a skeleton, with skin the color of dark chocolate. His head is clean-shaven, and buffed to a perfect shine. There is no way to tell how old he is.

"Did you have a time findin' tha place?" he asks. His voice is soothing, yet at the same time cold and slippery, like wet ice on a glass table.

"No," answers Nina. The truth is, she barely had to look for the place at all. It's as if she was drawn right to it.

The doctor has a huge cherrywood desk, spotlessly clean. His walls are covered with diplomas and certificates from the best universities and finest medical associations. He folds his long fingers together and sits at his giant desk across from Nina, smiling.

"Just what kind of doctor are you?" asks Nina.

"I began as a surgeon," Dr. Voyd tells her. "A brilliant one, oh, yes. Surgical techniques have been named after me. I am in textbooks."

"But you're not a surgeon anymore?"

"I got bored with that kind of medicine," he tells her. "Too easy. No challenge. And where I come from, I have seen many things that science cannot explain." He smiles, revealing spotlessly white teeth. "That is the kind of medicine I practice now. The kind of medicine *you* need."

Nina can feel her knees shaking. "How do you know what kind of medicine I need?"

Dr. Voyd laughs deep and heartily. "These things are obvious to a trained professional like me," he tells her. Then he gets deadly serious. "You are unhappy with yourself. You are thinkin' there must be a way to change those features of yours. Those green eyes aren't green enough, maybe. Or your nose comes to too sharp a point. And then there's that unsightly blemish on your cheek. Am I right?"

Nina nods, entranced by the way this man has examined her soul the way another doctor might examine her throat.

"Well," he tells her, "I am in the business of makeovers."

Nina's heart pounds with anticipation. "You can fix my face?"

"Not just your face, but everythin'. I can give you a new look—a new feel. I can give you a new body." And with that he stands and ushers Nina to a door that opens up into his spacious house. Only it is not a house. It looks more like a hospital from the dark ages. Or a morgue.

The walls are painted black and covered with strange symbols Nina cannot read. Hanging from the ceiling are voodoo dolls, with a single pin piercing them through the heart . . . and beneath each doll is a body, lying on a narrow steel gurney. At least a dozen of them, their slow breathing the only sign that they are alive.

"Welcome," says Dr. Voyd, "to the Soul Exchange."

Nina steps into the room to get a good look at the people in there. They are not the most beautiful specimens of humanity. Very unattractive by Nina's standards.

"It's a simple procedure," explains Dr. Voyd. "I extract their souls and implant them into new, more desirable bodies."

"How come they're all so ugly?"

Dr. Voyd sighs. "Once my clients trade up, I sometimes get left with bodies no one wants."

Nina can understand that. It's just like at last month's cheerleader bake sale. The lousy cookies never sold—and here was a whole roomful of lousy cookies.

"But . . . I don't want any of these bodies."

Dr. Voyd smiles his toothy grin. "I have one coming in tomorrow that is perfect for you." Then he reaches into a folder, pulls out a wallet-sized photo, and presents it to Nina.

And the moment Nina sees the face in the picture, she knows it's right! The girl in the picture is about thirteen, like Nina—and perfect. Thick locks of wavy blonde hair. Smooth skin, a wonderful smile, in a photograph rich with bright colors. She is far more beautiful than Nina—or even Heather. Yes, this will be the perfect exchange.

"It is my policy," explains Dr. Voyd, "that if you agree to the exchange, you may take nothing with you. Your personal belongings, your money—all must go to whoever inherits your old body. You understand?"

Nina nods. It will be worth it. Now only one question remains.

"How much?" asks Nina.

"For you," says Dr. Voyd, "two hundred dollars."

Nina thinks about it and nods. "It's a deal."

During school the next day, the anticipation hangs heavy over Nina. That morning she had "borrowed" her mother's ATM card and taken out two hundred dollars, which she brought directly over to Dr. Voyd. The exchange is to take place at four o'clock in the afternoon, *sharp*.

Throughout the day, she keeps glancing at Heather and can barely contain her mocking laughter. *Ha!* she thinks. *Tomor-*

row I'll walk into school—everyone's eyes will turn away from Heather and turn to me!

By the end of the day, she can't keep it to herself anymore. She has to tell someone. On the way out of school, she pulls Brent aside.

"I want to show you something," she tells him. Then she ever so carefully pulls the picture of her new self out of her purse. "What do you think of her?" she asks him. "Don't you think she's beautiful?"

Brent's eyes go wide as he stares at the picture, then he looks at her worriedly. "Is this a trick question?" he asks.

"Just answer me; Do you think she's beautiful?"

"Well . . . yeah," he says. "But . . ."

"But what?"

Brent holds the picture closer. "Her hair's kind of goofy looking . . ."

Nina lets out an irritated puff of air. "Well, she can change her hair. That's easy."

Brent hands her back the tiny picture. "So, what's the point?" he asks.

Nina smiles slyly. "You'll see."

Four o'clock sharp. The wind blows through the thick sycamores, and the rustling leaves are so loud Nina can't hear herself think as she races down the street.

"Everything is prepared," says Dr. Voyd as Nina steps in. "Follow me."

They pass through the room full of unwanted bodies to a smaller back room, lined with a dark and gritty metal Nina guesses must be lead. A body lies on a stone slab, covered with a sheet from head to toe, and above it dangles a voodoo doll, pinned like the others through the heart. A second stone slab waits for Nina. Dr. Voyd closes the heavy leaden door, and it seals the room like a bank vault.

"Lie down, Nina," says the good doctor. "This will take only a little while."

Nina lies down and watches as the doctor takes another doll from a shelf, then comes toward her with scissors. She tenses, terrified of what he might do. He brings the scissors to her face, then moves them off to the side, snipping a lock of her ginger hair. Then he takes that hair and carefully sews it into the seam of the doll's cloth head, calmly humming to himself.

"Just about ready."

Nina tries to fill her mind with thoughts of the perfect face she will have. At last, Dr. Voyd takes a long hat pin with a round pearl-colored head and holds it in one hand, the doll in the other.

"Take a deep breath and hold it," he instructs. She does, then watches as he jams the pin through the doll's heart.

Sudden blackness colder than the dark side of the moon, and emptier than death.

Nina feels herself moving through the darkness. It could be a million miles, it could be a million years; time and space have no meaning now. The cold is unbearable, but she has no mouth to scream, until—

She gasps, a deep breath of air that rattles in her lungs, then opens her eyes to see the cloudy cloth that covers her face. She pulls it back, revealing a bright light above. Out of focus. Then the light is eclipsed by Dr. Voyd's dark round head.

"You can get up now. The exchange is complete."

Nina sits up, feeling achy and weary. She looks to the other stone slab, but her old body is not there.

"You were in transition for an hour," explains the doctor. "During that time, the other client took possession of your body, and left."

Nina reaches up to her face. It doesn't feel right. Something is wrong. Her face feels cracked and rough like elephant skin. There is something round and fuzzy on her chin. A hairy mole!

She looks at her hands and screams. But no one can hear her but the doctor in the leaden room.

Her hands are old. More than old—they are ancient: wrinkled and weak, covered with the age spots of thirty thousand sunrises.

Dr. Voyd smiles coldly. Mockingly. "Another satisfied customer," he says and hands her a mirror.

Nina is now the old woman—the same old woman who gave her the card. *This* was the body she has exchanged for her own!

"No!" shouts Nina, but her voice sounds frail and thin. "This can't be me."

"What's the matter?" says Dr. Voyd. "Mrs. Ditmeyer is a beautiful woman! Of course, not as young as she was in that picture. But beauty is ageless."

Now Nina understands why the hairstyle in the picture didn't seem right. Why the photograph's color seemed to be almost painted on.

"You can't do this to me!" she screams. "I'm only thirteen!"

"Correction," says the doctor calmly. "You *were* only thirteen."

She cries through her blurry aged eyes.

"Of course," says the doctor, "if you're not happy with Mrs. Ditmeyer, I could give you one of the people in the other room."

"I don't want any of them!" wails Nina. "I want someone young! Someone beautiful."

Dr. Voyd crosses his arms. "Well," he says. "I can make such an exchange for you, if you bring in a young subject to exchange with."

At last some hope! "Yes!" she cries. "I'll bring you someone as soon as I can!"

"And then of course there's my fee," explains Dr. Voyd. "To put you in a young body ... that will cost you an even million dollars."

She gasps for air, her breath taken away by the mere thought.

"But I don't have a million dollars!"

Dr. Voyd puts a large firm hand on her shoulder. "Come now, Mrs. Ditmeyer. Of course you do! Have you checked your bank account lately?"

An early fall day, several weeks later. The old woman feeds pigeons in the park, all the while looking sideways at a group of loud young kids. Faces she recognizes. She wears jewelry so heavy she can barely lift her hands. But she does. She lifts one to her cane and painfully forces herself to her feet, making her way down the cobblestones to the group of kids.

Her former body is there, with someone new inside it. Brent, and Heather are there as well. They laugh and make fun of anyone who walks by. The kids see her coming and start to laugh hysterically.

"Here comes your last girlfriend," says the Nina-body to Brent. Brent thinks it's just a joke.

The old woman hobbles forward, her weary eyes fixed on Heather. She takes a card out of her pocket and holds it out to the gorgeous young girl with her trembling old hand.

"I've been watching you," says the old woman desperately to Heather. "I know a doctor who can help you. He can make you look even better than you do now. He knows what you need."

The Nina-body laughs cruelly as if it is one big joke. She

can afford to laugh; she is no longer trapped in Mrs. Dit-meyer's body.

Heather looks at the card with disgust and hands it back to the old woman. "Thanks, but no thanks," says Heather. And then she smiles. "I've already been to Dr. Voyd. In fact, I was there before you were."

The Nina-body laughs again. In fact, both girls laugh; evil and cold, like two members of a dark and secret club.

The old woman feels dizzy. She begins to fall backward, and Brent catches her. "Hey, are you okay?"

He helps her up, and she shrugs him off. "I'll be fine," she says and limps away, not daring to look back.

So Heather had been a client. Of course! She should have known! The fact was, Nina had come to realize that there had been many, many others who had been through Mrs. Dit-meyer's body. She was certainly a rich old woman. When the whole thing began, a year ago, she had fifteen million dollars according to her bankbook. Then about once a month, she wrote a check for a million dollars—always to Dr. Voyd, as different people were tricked into her body and bought their way out. It's like a game of musical chairs, and every turn costs a cool million—until someday soon the money will run out, and someone will get trapped in poor Mrs. Ditmeyer's chair for good.

Voyd is a genius. And now he is very, very rich. She admires him almost as much as she hates him.

As she makes her way toward her decaying mansion across Central Park, someone comes running up behind her.

"Yo, old lady, wait up!"

It's Brent.

"What can I do for you, young man?"

"That doctor you're talking about," he says. "Is he a doctor for guys too? I mean, can he make a guy better looking too?"

The old woman looks him over slowly. This is something she has not considered. "Perhaps," she says, then reaches into her pocket and pulls out the card, handing it to him.

"I think he'll know what you need, too," she says. "Call him for an appointment right away."

"Thanks," says Brent with a big smile. Then he turns and runs off.

The old woman grins at the new prospect. It's not what she expected—and of course there will be many, many adjustments . . . like getting used to the wrestling team for one—and then there's the problem of dating her old self.

But she'll learn to adapt, because, in spite of everything, his youth is certainly worth a million dollars. And beggars can't be choosers.

DAMIEN'S SHADOW

● ●

With power beating through my muscles, I drove around Max, controlling the basketball with such incredible skill it seemed to be a part of me. On the sidelines, music pounded out a rhythm with the same intensity that my ball pounded the rhythm on the pavement. It was starting to get late, but the heat of the day had not yet given way to the comfortable cool of a late summer evening. I knew the hour by the length of my shadow, stretched across the asphalt, making my legs look even longer, like a real basketball player's, and making my arms seem monstrous, like the arms of a spider.

I drove around Max, around Jason; I even got past their center who was so tall and broad everyone just called him Tree. I broke for the basket! With my powerful feet, I flew into the air, and once airborne left my shadow orphaned on the pavement. With the ball cupped in my hand, held there as if by a magnet, I swung it toward the basket. I was not tall enough to dunk, but I could bounce it off the backboard like a pro and get it right into the net.

Then as I released it from my fingers, out of nowhere a hand eclipsed the light in my face, smashing the ball back into my nose. I saw a bright flash before I felt the pain, which came sharp and jagged. I tumbled and was down once again, meeting my shadow in a bone-bruising hug on the concrete. Cupping my hands to my nose, I cursed. My nose was not broken—at least I didn't think it was—but it was bleeding. I stood up trying to fight the pain, trying to pretend it didn't hurt. Then I screamed at that sycamore of a center, "Goaltending, you moron!"

My best friend Max—who also happened to be my greatest adversary when it came to basketball—just shrugged.

"It wasn't goaltending. You weren't close enough to the basket for it to be goaltending."

"What are you talking about, I was right up there!" I yelled.

I brought up my shirt and dabbed the drops of blood coming from my nose. I looked to my own teammates. They backed me up—they pointed fingers at Max and their choose-up teammates.

"You guys cheat like there's no tomorrow!" I said.

Max crossed his arms. "Are we gonna play, or are we gonna stand here picking each other's noses?" And he whacked the wagging fingers out of his face. My teammates backed down and just shook their heads.

"C'mon, we're still winning," I said, which was true.

It was then that I saw something strange. At first I didn't think much of it. My shadow was long and dark, cast by the setting sun. Although I made no move, I saw my shadow reach out and slap Max's shadow hard on the back. I saw Max's shadow stumble, then recover.

When I blinked, both shadows were exactly where they should have been, and I wondered if it was just a trick of the light, or if perhaps I was getting sunstroke from playing basketball for too long in the heat of the day. I thought nothing of it until the following day.

Summer school.

Day after day of math and science, math and science. Not the summer school you might think. I was there by choice. I wasn't there to make up for work I didn't do, but to get ahead on work I didn't want to do next year. I had always been a good student and a good athlete, too. I was competitive in everything I did, and I *always* won. When they said that I might be able to skip eighth grade by doing extra work during the summer, I knew it was a challenge I wanted to take. I knew it was a game I could win.

"You're just not smart enough," said Melanie, who was taking the summer classes with me. She was always first in class, getting A's and A-pluses in everything that she did. I liked Melanie almost as much as I hated her. It was good having her around because it kept me on my toes.

"You're just dumb," she said as we worked through math equations. "It's a fact: boys are dumb—girls are smarter. No matter what, I'll always get higher grades than you."

I gritted my teeth and sneered at her. "Don't count on it, Melonhead." I turned back to my work, concentrated on the numbers, and tried to solve the equations faster. I processed those numbers in my brain at the highest speed that I could and was about to announce the answer when Melanie shouted it out.

"Forty-two," she said. "X equals forty-two."

"Very good, Melanie," said the teacher. I pounded my fist on the table, and the teacher turned to me laughing. "Gotta be a little bit faster, Damien."

Melanie smiled her superior smile at me. I was so angry that my eyes were about to tear. I looked away, catching sight of the shadow of my head against the cabinet. I could see my profile, my nose elongated, my lips, my hand.

My hand . . .

I held my hand up and moved my fingers, remembering what I had seen on the basketball court yesterday. The shadow-fingers moved along with me. I put my hand down . . . but my shadow-fingers did not go down. I saw them grab Melanie's shadow by the hair. I watched as another hand came up and around the neck of Melanie's shadow. I saw Melanie's shadow begin to struggle—and all I could do was stare, slack jawed.

"What are you looking at, dweeb?" I snapped my eyes to Melanie, who was staring at me as if I was from outer space.

"Just the wall," I said. "Is it against the law to look at the wall?"

When I turned to the shadows again I still saw it just as clearly as before. My shadow held Melanie's shadow tightly by the neck until Melanie's fell into a heap, just a clump of gray light where the wall met the floor. It stayed there like a discoloration in the green linoleum tile, and I imagined that the dead, dark spot would never wash away. I shivered.

"Damien," Melanie said to me, this time a little bit more worried than before. "Are you all right?"

I guess my eyes must have peeled way too wide. "Yeah, yeah, I'm fine," I said. Then I asked her what she saw when she looked at the wall.

"Just your shadow," she said with a shrug.

"Me too." I raised my hand and wiggled my fingers. My shadow did exactly what it was supposed to do. When we were done with our assignment we left the room. I never mentioned to Melanie what she should have noticed about herself: She saw my shadow, but she did not see hers.

The news was out by the next morning. Gossip traveled through our neighborhood like a scent on the wind, and the day's gossip was about Melanie Defalco.

"Did you hear?" shouted a neighbor to my mother as she came out to pick up the newspaper. "Melanie Defalco ran away."

"Ran away?" my mother said.

I shook my head. "No way, Melanie's not the kind of girl that runs away. The only thing she'd run away from would be a bad grade."

But as I walked around the neighborhood that morning and listened to what people had to say, it seemed clear that Melanie was gone. For most of the morning I had completely blocked out what I had seen in the classroom the day before. See, there are things you deal with every day, and there are some things you keep to yourself not because you want to but because you have to—because nobody, not the people who love you the most, not even your closest friends, would ever believe you.

What I saw or what I *thought* I saw, I kept to myself for a long time. Each day I went to school and prayed that Melanie would show up, but she didn't. And every time that I caught sight of my shadow, in stark sunlight or in the faint incandescent glow of a single lightbulb, I shuddered. It seemed so innocent. Always doing what it was expected to do while I was looking. But then every once in a while it would make a move that looked slightly wrong—that was slightly different from what I had done. But I'd tell myself that it was my imagination.

A week after Melanie disappeared, I spent an afternoon over at Max's house reading comic books, talking about sports—and girls. We spent a whole half hour trying to figure out the best way one might ask out Sondra Marsh, whom all the guys liked, but no one dared date.

I guess it was our talk about girls that got Max thinking about Melanie.

"You think she'll ever come back?" asked Max.

I didn't answer him. I knew it would be a disaster to say anything. But even disaster would be better than what was going on inside my head just then.

"Max," I said quietly. "Have you ever taken a look at your shadow? I mean, really taken a look at it?"

"My shadow?" He thought about it and shrugged. "Sure, I guess. I mean, it's just my shadow."

"Yeah," I said to him. "But what if it wasn't *just* your shadow? What if it had ideas of its own? What if it had the power to do some of the things that you thought about doing in your darkest dreams, but wouldn't dare in real life."

Max returned his attention to his comic book. "Get real!" he said.

I pulled the comic away from him, and it tore. I thought that he'd get mad at me but instead he just looked at me strangely, like I was from the moon.

"Damien? What's up with you, huh?"

I tried to pick my words very carefully, arranging them in my head before I spoke them out loud.

"Max," I said. "I think something's happening to me. But it's not just me. It's happening to people around me, too. People . . . like Melanie." I could almost see a wall fall between us as I spoke. Max backed up.

"What about Melanie?"

"My shadow strangled hers," I told him.

Max looked around, picked up his torn comic book, and headed toward the door.

"Listen, I gotta go," he said.

"This is your house," I reminded him.

Max took it in stride and nodded. "Right. Well, I gotta go anyway." And he left me alone in his living room. So much for my best friend.

The next morning I smoothed the whole thing over, doing my best to convince Max that it was just a joke that he took too seriously. Then, at summer school, I didn't talk to anyone all morning. I even ate lunch alone, in the corner of the cafeteria. The fluorescent lights above gave off an even, diffused light—the kind of light that is flat and smooth and casts no shadows. It was the kind of light I tried to hide myself in these days. I sat there moving my semi-liquefied beans back and forth on my Styrofoam plate, trying to make my over-achieving brain figure out some way to control my shadow. Is there a way to grab it? Is there a way to hold it? And if I could, what might it feel like in my hand? Would it feel light and airy like a black silk stocking or would it feel cold and empty like a swirling winter wind? I would probably never know because whenever I tried to reach for it, it would reach away, copying my moves precisely until the moment I stopped looking.

The thing about isolating yourself in a huge cafeteria is that suddenly you become a target—suddenly you get noticed, even if disappearing is what you are really trying to do.

Someone sat down across from me. When I looked up my

heart stopped painfully suspended between beats. It was Sondra Marsh. Of all the times for Sondra Marsh to come up and talk to me, why did it have to be today?

"Hi," she said. "You looked lonely. I thought you might want some company."

I shrugged, barely even daring to look at her. "I'm not lonely," I told her. "Just alone."

She went on talking about how she hated having to take summer school science and how she wished she could have brains like me. "Maybe, if we have some of the same classes in the fall, we could study together," she suggested.

"Yeah, sure," I told her, trying not to sound overly enthusiastic. "Yeah, that'd be great." It's amazing how girls have the power to wipe a guy's mind clean. Suddenly I couldn't remember what I had been thinking about before she'd gotten there.

She smiled at me again. "It was nice talking with you, Damien." Then she got up and left.

The cafeteria was clearing out now, everybody getting ready to go home since summer school was only half days. I watched Sondra leave, and before I knew what I was doing I was up on my feet and hurrying after her. I just couldn't leave it alone. I had to push forward, just like I did in the classroom, just like I did on the court. I never waited for success at anything; I always pushed it. I had never been pushy with girls, but this time I had been handed the ball. I couldn't keep myself from driving down the line.

I caught up with her just outside the school gate.

"Sondra," I called.

She turned and smiled just as the sun came out from behind a cloud, making it seem as if her smile had lit up the sun.

"Sondra, you doing anything tonight?" I asked.

She shrugged. "Nothing special."

"I was thinking of going to the movies," I told her. "Maybe you'd like to come?"

She had no hesitation. "Yeah, that'd be nice," she said.

Suddenly I realized that I had done too good a job catching up with her and that I was standing a little too close. Embarrassed I looked down to see our shadows short and squat in the midday sun against the pebble-marked concrete.

My shadow was kissing hers.

The sight stupefied me, and all I could do was look up at Sondra, gaping.

"What's wrong?" she asked.

"Nothing, nothing," I covered. "I'm just glad about going to the movie together, you know?"

She took me for my word and left saying "See you tonight." I looked down as her shadow pulled away from mine and left with her.

I knew that I could never let her shadow meet mine again, so instead of going to the movies that night, I found a broken-down basketball court that no one wanted to use and played by myself, trying to lock my mind on my layups. I went home when it got too dark to see on the court—too dark to have a shadow—and I stayed out of streetlights all the way home.

But at night, when I was alone in my room, sitting at the head of my bed, I couldn't get the shadow out of my mind. The moonlight painted a sharp-edged shadow against my closet door of the tree outside my window. The long and twisted bough seemed like an octopus tentacle, and I kept on expecting it to move.

I reached out my hand into the moonlight, daring to catch a shadow on the wall. Five fingers, so much darker than my own and just as powerful. Then I dared do something I had been afraid to from the very beginning. Quickly, impulsively, I threw my hand to the wall, grasping at my shadow . . .

. . . And I actually caught it! I held it, but only for a second. I felt it slip out of my fingers like a snakeskin.

So, I said to it, *you can be caught.*

It was a glimmer of hope, and I held on to that glimmer as I fell asleep.

Nothing could have prepared me for what happened next. It was one of those strange twists of fate that damns everyone it touches. It turned out that Sondra went to the movies looking for me, but instead found Max. From what I was able to find out, they never went into the movie. Instead they went to get a burger and talk. They talked a lot. They got to know each other a lot better—and the next day I saw them walking down the street, much too close to one another.

I said "Hi" as I passed them, and didn't dare look at them. Only Max said "hi" back, his nose up in the air, like a proud victor. After all, he had wanted to go out with Sondra as much as I had. I kept walking, determined not to look back, but I felt my feet start to drag as if my shoes had suddenly become lead weights. It wasn't my shoes. Tall and thin in the morning sun, my shadow stretched behind me, trying to crawl away from me like a spider, trying to crawl to them. I picked up my pace and dragged it away.

At home, I closed the door to my room, pulled the curtains, and shoved blankets in the cracks. Then, when my eyes had adjusted to the dim light, I took a roll of masking tape and sealed out the light coming from around the door frame. I unplugged the digital clock and sat alone in absolute darkness. I knew a shadow couldn't exist without the light to create it, and

I wondered if it was possible to live the rest of my life in total darkness.

Max showed up later that afternoon. I heard him ring the bell. I heard his muffled call up to the window.

Maybe he'll go away, I said to myself. But best friends don't go away. He must have found an open window, because he found his way in and creaked open my door, flipping on the light. I must have looked like a vampire as I sat there on the bed, squinty eyed.

"What are you sleeping for? It's the middle of the day!" he said.

"You don't want to be here, Max. Just go."

"You're mad at me because of Sondra, aren't you?" he said. "Well, you had your chance. You're the one who stood her up."

I felt my hands ball up into fists. How could he be so stupid to think that all of this could be just because of that?

"I don't want to hurt you," I told him.

He looked at me, jutting his jaw out. "What's that supposed to mean? You want to fight me, is that what you're saying?"

"No, no, no!" I screamed at him. I reached out and pushed him hard, trying to get him out the door.

"You've got problems," he yelled, and then he yelled a whole lot of other things. But I didn't hear his words—I was too busy watching my shadow, which had already crossed paths with his. See, there's this plastic sword leaned up against the corner of my room. It's just a stupid prop from a school play I was in, but I've always kept it because it looked kind of cool. Max kept talking on and on while I watched my shadow grab the shadow of the sword . . . and mercilessly run Max's shadow through!

I screeched as my shadow pulled out the sword. Max's

shadow crumbled to the ground and lay there, leaving the same gray stain that Melanie's had left.

"And one more thing," continued Max. "You stink at basketball, too!"

He turned and stormed out.

I knew I couldn't just leave it like that—I didn't know exactly what would happen to him, but I still had to warn him!

I caught up with him on the street and forced him to stop and listen.

"Max, remember when I was talking to you about the shadows?" I said to him.

"Yeah, what about it?"

"I want you to look at yours." Max was the kind of guy who didn't believe a thing unless he saw it. He looked down. The afternoon sun was bright, casting my shadow on the concrete. Where his shadow should have been there was nothing; only unbroken sunlight. He looked at it for a long time. He didn't get scared. Not yet.

"So what's the trick?" he asked.

"No trick," I told him. "Your shadow is dead. I watched it die."

But I suppose even seeing wasn't believing this time. He hardened his gaze.

"I don't have time for this noise," he told me and walked off, looking at the ground, at his feet, at his arms, and everywhere around him for the slightest trace of his shadow.

I skipped dinner. I told my mom that I had a stomachache and sat alone in my room and watched TV, trying to lose my mind to the blaring box.

Max came by around eight o'clock that night. I don't know what had gone through his mind between when he left me on the street and the moment he showed up at my door, but whatever it was, it had left him tired and terrified. He asked if he could spend the night at my house—a sleep-over—like we had when we were younger.

We sat together watching TV. The early evening shows and the late evening shows, the news and the late late movies. Then we played board games, long after my mother had gone to bed, long after the moon had set in the sky. We sat there keeping each other awake, terrified of what might happen to Max if he fell asleep.

"Maybe it's not going to happen to me," said Max at around three in the morning. "Maybe if I stay awake, the sun will come and will give me a new shadow."

"Maybe," I said. For after all, he had gone this long and he was still here. Maybe knowing it was about to happen would keep it from happening. I tried to stay awake, but my eyelids dropped and my consciousness fell away from me, as if it had fallen through a trapdoor. I remembered no dreams. I remembered no time passing—until I was woken by a desperate whisper at dawn.

"Damien! Damien, help me!"

I snapped my eyes awake. The first rays of dawn were pouring through the room, creating shafts of light filled with floating dust. I watched as the light passed through the air and shone on Max's unbelieving face. If you have ever seen a person vanish from existence, and I doubt that you have, it's not something that happens all at once. It takes a while—seven minutes to be exact. The amount of time it takes the sun to break over the horizon.

Max lost his dimension first, not all of them, just one. As I looked at him, he seemed to go flat against the wall. I reached up to touch him, but instead banged my hand against the plaster. He was a flat projection against the white wall of my room.

"Do something, Damien. I'm afraid!" he cried.

But how can you help a projection? As the sun peaked higher above the horizon, his color went next. His bright blue shirt faded, and all his colors became different shades of gray like an old black-and-white TV. The sound of his sobs became more and more muffled as all the grays of his form began to swirl and merge together, the hard lines dissolving into one another, like a stain washing out of a wet rag.

"I'm sorry, Max," I whispered woefully. "I'm so sorry . . ."

In a moment, there was only a dull shape where he had been, and in a moment more, it faded completely, leaving nothing but a daylight-painted wall.

That was yesterday.

In the neighborhood, people are still trying to figure out what happened to Max. The police questioned my mom and me. I told them that he must have disappeared sometime during the night.

There'll be more questions, I'm sure—but that doesn't matter anymore.

It's night again. Outside the moon shines bright. Mom stayed up late after the trouble-filled day, but finally dozed off around midnight. As for me, I'm staying up all night.

I don't need to worry about my shadow anymore. It's not going to hurt anyone. Because now it hangs from the shadow of the tree limb, against my closet door. It was hard to catch, and harder still to loop the shadow of the rope around its neck, but in the end I won. I always win.

Amazing to think that the limp blotch dangling against my closet door could have caused so much trouble. But I can rest easy, knowing that it will never bother anyone ever again.

So I'll wait out the night, playing board games alone and listening to the ticking of the clock. It was a fine thing to beat my shadow at its own game. Now all I have to do is beat the dawn.

TERRIBLE TANNENBAUM

• •

Endless rows of pine trees stretched as far as the eye could see, all pruned to a perfect point. It was Christmas again, and Tammy McDaniels trekked with her parents and brothers to select this year's tree.

"See all these trees," said Brett, Tammy's older brother. "Well, in six weeks, they'll all be dead."

Eight-year-old Michael, Tammy's younger brother, stared at Brett with wide-eyed shock. Apparently he had never thought of such a thing—that trees could live and die like people.

"That's right," continued Brett. "They'll all be axed so that we can have presents under a tree." Brett gave his little brother a nasty smile. "Merry Christmas."

"Brett, kindly keep your thoughts on the subject to yourself," said Dad.

Tammy, who was almost twelve, wasn't bothered anymore

by the things Brett said. But it did bother her to see Michael tormented so.

"Will you look at this one," said Mom as she pushed through the pine branches of the lot. "This is a healthy one."

"Too small," said Dad.

"How about this one?" said Michael.

"Too thin."

"How about that one?" said Tammy.

"Too fat."

"Gimme a break," said Brett. "What is this, 'Goldilocks and the Three Trees'?"

"Brett," said Mom, "why don't you just go sit in the car."

"Are you kidding," mocked Brett. "I'm having too much fun."

It was easy for Tammy to ignore Brett. She had grown used to him and his sick sense of humor. And anyway, she had her *own* philosophy when it came to Christmas trees. To Tammy, the trees on the lot were grown for one purpose only: to celebrate Christmas. Naturally, it was what the trees lived for. If a Christmas tree did have a spirit, Tammy knew it wanted to be taken from the lot and brought into a warm home where it could be adorned and surrounded by love. Each Christmas, Tammy could feel the goodwill breathing from those happy trees. She wondered if there were ever any Christmas trees that didn't feel that way.

Brett, however, never got into the Christmas spirit. When the family had purchased an aluminum tree one Christmas, he had complained that it was tacky. "How silly," he had said, "to have a tree made of metal." To Brett, it had been as ridiculous as the pink plastic flamingo Mom maintained on the front lawn. Then, when the family decided to buy a live tree, Brett complained that they were brutally killing a tree just to celebrate Christmas. As if that weren't enough, each year on Christmas morning Brett would pout that he never got what he wanted, even when he got exactly what he wanted.

It had become a family tradition that all of them go to the U-Cut Christmas tree lot and pick out a tree, even though everyone would rather Brett stay home, including Brett.

"By the way," said Brett, "don't count on Santa coming this year. There's no such thing as Santa."

Michael's lower lip started to quiver. True, Michael was getting a little old to believe in Santa, thought Tammy, but just because he did believe didn't mean that Brett had to tease him about it.

"You take that back!" screamed Michael.

"Brett," said Dad, "it's bad enough you pull the wings off of flies. Do you have to torture your poor brother, too?"

"Make him take it back," bawled Michael.

"Take it back, Brett," warned Mom, "if you know what's good for you."

"Fine, fine," said Brett. "I take it back. There is a Santa Claus, okay? He comes down our chimney every single year with nice gifts for all the good little boys and girls, and he does lunch with the Easter Bunny in the off-seasons. Are you happy now?"

Michael stopped crying, and Mom sighed with relief.

"Santa knows you're a good boy, Michael," she said—but said no such thing to Brett.

They pushed their way through hundreds of trees until they lost all sense of direction. Tammy played hide-and-seek with Michael, hidden in the dense forest of evenly spaced trees. Michael would occasionally get lost and cry until someone found him—but that was all part of the fun. Dad forged on, holding the heavy ax by its neck until they came to a little bald spot in the tree farm. In the center of that bald spot stood what looked like a single perfect tree. It wasn't until the family got closer that they realized several unusual things. First, the tree was surrounded by a thin layer of snow, even though the first snow of the season had not yet fallen. Second, all the other trees on the edge of the bald spot were leaning away from this tree in the center. It looked like they were actually growing away from it.

If trees had legs, thought Tammy, they might be running away.

"Well, isn't that odd," said Mom.

"Not at all," said Dad, "trees don't always grow straight."

It was cold inside that clearing, colder than anywhere else on the tree farm. Mom zipped up her jacket and made sure Tammy and Michael's were zipped as well.

"Cold front coming in," said Dad.

Brett stepped up to the tree and reached into it to see if there was any rot.

"Ouch," he said and quickly withdrew his hand. He had pricked his finger on a pine needle.

"I don't like this tree," said Brett. "It has an attitude."

But if any of them had reservations about the tall, lonely pine, those reservations were wiped away when they saw the price tagged onto one of its lower limbs: eight dollars. The tree was eight feet tall, and any of the other eight-foot trees went for at least fifty bucks.

Dad was overjoyed. But Tammy was feeling more and more unsettled by the tree. A tree shouldn't make a person feel that way, she thought.

"Maybe," said Tammy, "the people who run the tree farm know something we don't. Maybe that's why it's priced so low."

"Nonsense," said Dad, hefting the heavy ax he used only once a year. "They must have mispriced it by mistake and I'm not going to pass up a bargain like that." He swung the ax low.

THWACK. The heavy head of the ax buried itself deep in the tree's soft, wet wood. He pried it out and swung again.

THWACK. The tree groaned and creaked; the cold wind blew stronger. The surrounding trees seemed to take on a greater tilt away.

THWACK. At last the tree could hold on no longer.

TIMBER! Severed from its roots, the tree collapsed down, its branches flopping to the side.

"We're going to have a fine Christmas," said Mom.

"The best ever," said Dad.

"Another one bites the dust," said Brett.

And the tree said absolutely nothing.

At home they sawed the base smooth and wrestled the tree onto the large stand, where an iron spike dug itself deep up into the tree's trunk.

Ten minutes later the tree had already started to tilt. No one seemed to notice since they were busy hanging ornaments. First, they hung the lights. Then came the glass ornaments. Next, the special ornaments: baby's first Christmas, first Christmas together, and the like. They adorned the tree till its outer branches were shining and beautiful . . . while deep within, the twisted branches remained dark.

It was by far the tallest tree they'd ever had. Eight feet did not look that big on the lot, but here in the house, even with its vaulted ceilings, the tree seemed huge and imposing. When the family finished trimming the tree, Mom sat at the piano, and they gathered 'round. As was family tradition, they sang "O Tannenbaum"—which none of the kids could sing with a straight face, as this was what they always sang to tease Joey Tannenbaum, who lived across the street.

It wasn't until after they were done that they noticed how cold it was getting in the house, although the heater was turned on full blast. Even Moby, their goldfish, seemed to shiver in his bowl on the piano. They decided to have a fire, which warmed the fireplace, but little else.

"It's the humidity," said Dad.

"Bad insulation," said Mom.

But it was Michael who was first to suspect the truth.

"It's the tree," he said.

Tammy and the others looked over to him, as he stood next to the tree.

"That's odd," said Mom. The tree seemed to be leaning toward Michael.

"It doesn't like us," said Michael.

The way Tammy saw it, the tree wasn't just leaning—it was looming. Looming over Michael like a tidal wave waiting to crash.

"Get real," said Brett.

Tammy went over to the tree and put her hand near it. It did seem colder near the tree than anywhere else. Tammy thought to reach her hand into that tree, but then changed her mind. There should be some light in there from all of those lights strung around the outside of the tree, she thought. Why was the inside of the tree so dark? She turned to her parents.

"Weird," she said, but they both shrugged. Then she felt something soft and spiny like a caterpillar rub up against her arm. She gasped and slapped it away.

But it was only a bough of pine needles.

She was about to laugh, until she realized that she was not the one who had moved closer to the tree. *It was the tree that had brushed against her!*

A red ornament jangled ominously on the branch.

"Smile, sweetie!"

A bright light flashed in her face as Mom snapped a picture of her beside the tree. Did the tree flinch at the flash, or was it just Tammy's imagination? She couldn't be sure—but there was one thing she *was* sure of: this tree, unlike any other tree she had known, had no feeling of Christmas love and goodwill.

That night, after the fire had burned out, the only glow came from the multicolored lights of the Christmas tree. They cast spiny shadows of red, blue, and green on the white walls.

Brett was in his room being antisocial, and before Tammy went to sleep she went in to give him a piece of her mind.

"What are you doing in here?" challenged Brett. "I thought you were downstairs sucking in some Christmas spirit."

"Brett," she said, "sometimes you're such a creep. Just because you don't like Christmas doesn't mean you have to ruin it for the rest of us . . . telling Michael there is no Santa, and all."

"Why should you care?" said Brett. "Maybe I'm trying to protect him—maybe I don't want him to be disappointed later."

"Maybe you just like to make people feel lousy." Tammy turned to leave but just as she reached the door, Brett said something that made her stop.

"There is a Santa Claus."

Tammy turned back. "What?"

"I said, there really is a Santa Claus."

"Shut up, Brett. I don't like it when you tease me."

"Who said I was teasing?" Brett was looking down at the video game he was playing. He paused the game for a moment and looked at Tammy.

"He can fit down the chimney 'cause he doesn't have any collarbones. His reindeer fly because nobody told them that they can't. He gets to every kid's house 'cause he knows how to stop time and travel in between the seconds. And every once in a while when he finds a bad kid, a *really* bad kid, he wakes him up in the middle of the night and tells him, 'Hey son, I'm sorry, but you don't get a gift from me this year 'cause you've been way too naughty.' Just like he said to me when I was nine." Brett shrugged "And I guess I've just been naughty ever since."

Tammy stood there for a minute, almost taking it seriously. Then she shook it off.

"Ha ha," said Tammy. "Very funny."

"Laugh all you want," said Brett, "but that's why I don't like Christmas, and I hope someday Santa gets his."

Downstairs, their father unplugged the Christmas tree lights and the whole house was plunged into pine-scented darkness.

At three in the morning, everyone was awoken by a heavy THUD and the tinkling of breaking glass. It was the kind of dead-of-night sound that brought terror to any household.

"Daddy," Tammy wailed, "someone's breaking in!"

Tammy came out of her room to see Dad racing downstairs with a baseball bat—all set to do battle with a burglar. He flipped on the light . . . but there were no burglars. In an instant it became clear what had intruded into their night: The tree had fallen onto the piano, leaving shattered glass ornaments all over the keys.

The fear that had woken Tammy up still raged inside. She kept telling herself that it was just a fallen tree, but it didn't quiet the uneasy feeling that pounded through her. There was something about the sight that was terrible—like a car wreck.

Michael, who was peering down through the banister, began to cry.

"I don't like that tree, Daddy," he whimpered.

"It's okay, Michael," said Mom, "we'll fix it in the morning."

She and Dad lifted the tree off the piano. Pieces of broken

Christmas ornaments rained to the ground. Baby's first Christmas, first Christmas together. All smashed to bits.

"We'll have to get a new base," said Dad. The steel legs were horribly twisted out of shape. "Funny," said Dad, "they said it could hold a tree up to fifteen feet. Metal fatigue, I guess."

Then Tammy noticed that among the fine fragments of shattered ornaments were shards of glass much thicker than the rest.

"Moby!" she gasped. From behind the banister, Michael began to whimper harder.

"It's okay," said Dad, trying to exercise a little damage control. "We'll get a new fish tomorrow. Maybe we'll get two. Maybe a whole family—how's that?"

Michael settled down and Tammy helped her parents clean up the mess, and when they were done, Tammy stared at the tree until Dad turned out the light. Lying on its side, the branches of the tree all swayed down toward the ground—but somehow those branches seemed to be moving, squirming, and it occurred to her that they never did find Moby.

Tammy went to bed that night dreaming of a tree whose branches were octopus tentacles and whose trunk was the scaly body of a python.

By the time Christmas Eve arrived, the tree had fallen a total of five times. Dad had tethered it to the light hanging from the ceiling above it, and still it pulled loose from the cord. Now it was tied to three different spots in the room—the light above, the banister, and the upstairs railing. There was no way it was moving—it looked like King Kong in shackles. As for its trimming, they had given up on glass ornaments, since there were only two or three left. All that remained on the tree now were the unbreakable things—silver tinsel and popcorn chains. The walls in the corner of the living room were filled with gouges, and green marks from where the tree had fallen, as if some battle had taken place there.

Michael wouldn't even go into the living room anymore, and Dad joked that they would probably have to put their presents under the tree—literally *under* the tree—to prop it up.

"When's the Christmas tree burn this year, Dad?" Michael asked. Everyone knew Michael hated to see the trees burn, but this was one year he was actually looking forward to it.

Although he wouldn't admit it, even Brett steered clear of the psychotic pine as best he could.

It was Tammy who kept a close watch on the tree, puzzling over it. She imagined that if trees truly did have personalities, then a tree could be bad, the way some people might be bad.

She sat alone across from the tree as Christmas Eve faded into twilight. While everyone else watched *It's a Wonderful Life* in the family room, Tammy peered into its darkness— watching it the way a guard might watch a prisoner. Its limbs blew with the breeze, even though there was no breeze, and when she looked into it long enough, she could swear she saw faces in there, staring out at her, but she was certain it was just her imagination. Why did they have to take this tree? Why couldn't they have chosen a tree that *wanted* to be a part of the celebration, as did all the trees they had in the past? Trees that weren't selfish. Or evil.

"I'll bet Santa will come and take it away," said Michael, peering in from the hallway. "Santa would never let a tree like that ruin Christmas."

It took a long time for Tammy to fall asleep that Christmas Eve. She kept thinking about what gifts the morning would bring, but mostly she thought about the tree.

In her dreams, the tree, with its snake trunk and octopus arms, spoke to her in a slippery whisper of a voice.

"Have yourself a Merry Little Christmas," the dream-tree told her, then wrapped its tentacles around her and pulled her into its darkness.

Christmas dawn was frigid. Cold drafts had blown down the open flue of the chimney, filling the house with icy winter air and fireplace ash.

Tammy awoke to the sound of bells jingling somewhere outside and met her brothers just coming out of their rooms farther down the hall. Not even the icy cold could blunt the joy of Christmas morning, thought Tammy. Not even the tree. Tammy smiled as she and her brothers reached the edge of the stairs.

"I know Santa brought me a new bike!" said Michael.

"I'll bet I got a whole mess of video games," said Tammy.

"I'll probably get stupid clothes that don't fit," said Brett.

And with that, they clambered down the stairs.

Brett saw it before Tammy did. He gasped, and his face became as green as the Christmas cookies they had eaten the night before.

Santa, it turned out, had indeed come.

Michael instantly began to cry and buried his face in Brett's chest. Brett, who normally would just push him away, held Michael tight. Tammy could only gape. Holding onto the banister, she felt as if her legs would buckle beneath her.

The tree had fallen sometime in the dead of night. This time it didn't engulf the piano. Instead it pinned one brightly dressed, bearded old man to the hardwood floor.

Outside the sleigh bells impatiently jangled, and deer hooves restlessly scraped the roof.

Where were Mom and Dad? thought Tammy. Had they

drank so much eggnog last night that they were sleeping through this?

The man trapped beneath the tree turned his head weakly and spoke in a raspy, wheezy voice.

"Muh-muh-merry Chr-Chr-Chr—"

Tammy looked to Brett. The corners of Brett's mouth had turned up in a sinister, Grinch-like grin. He raced off into the garage and returned moments later with their father's ax. Then he looked at the man beneath the tree.

"I've had about enough of you," he said, as he raised the ax high above his head.

"No!" screamed Tammy. She grabbed Michael, turning his head so he wouldn't see.

The blade came down and sank deep into the dark trunk of the tree. From the tree came a hideous wailing cry.

"Watch out!" warned Brett. He swung again. Pine sap splattered in all directions, leaving thick, sticky clumps in Tammy's hair. A third swing. *Thwok!* Then a fourth. *Thwok!* The tree shattered, its limbs tangled around the ax, but Brett pulled it free and raised the ax high above his head one last time.

"You're sawdust!" he said, and with that brought down the blade for a final blow that split the terrible tree in two, freeing the not-so-jolly man trapped beneath.

Michael and Tammy helped him up. Brett, dropping the ax to the ground with a thud, stared the silver-haired visitor in the face.

"Well," said Brett. "What am I now? Naughty or nice?"

"Please, I'm in no mood," said Santa. He turned to look up at the closed door of their parents' room. "Tell your parents to stay away from cheap trees. You get what you pay for." And with that he turned to go.

"Thankless old man," grumbled Brett beneath his breath— but apparently nothing escaped the man's large, pink ears.

Santa turned back to Brett. "Very well," he said reluctantly, tossing Brett a small box. "I suppose you've earned it. It's in the driveway."

Inside the box Brett found a key.

"And Brett," said Santa Claus. "Do stop being such a royal pain, or I'll have to send the tooth fairy to punch out some of those pearly whites."

Once their guest had made his exit, they bundled up the remains of the tree and Tammy set it on fire in the backyard. She watched as it burned with a furious flame, its darkness completely consumed and reduced to ashes in a matter of minutes. Then, she set up the old aluminum tree.

In the end, Tammy had to admit that Christmas morning turned out the same as always—for by the time Mom and Dad finally dragged themselves out of bed, the house was clean and there was nothing out of the ordinary to explain.

Nothing, that is, but the Porsche in the driveway.

DEAD LETTER

••

Tomb it may concern,

I have, for much too long, suffered from the insults, cruel attacks, and blatant discrimination in your newspaper. As the only newspaper in the town of Rancid Falls, one might think you would learn to be fair and objective with the items you report. But in fact, in your paper, my kind have been treated with more disrespect than we can stand.

Haven't you ever heard the expression "show respect for the dead"? I suppose not! Let me tell you, it makes quite a few of us roll over in our graves—as you can probably tell from that rumbling sound you occasionally hear from the graveyard on the hill.

Oh sure, you write all these nice, flowery notes the day we go on to our final rest—but the second we try to return from the grave, we are no longer welcome. Suddenly those sweet flowery things you've written become big banner headlines, turning our simple homecomings into horrible events, as if we were criminals.

For instance: Your headline last week read CORPSE TERRORIZES FAMILY. I would hardly call climbing in through a window in the middle of the night and playing Beethoven on the family piano an act of terror. If the woman fainted and the children ran screaming down the street, that's their problem, don't you think?

A week before that, you ran a headline that read HEADLESS WOMAN CARJACKS CADILLAC. As if it had been her intent to steal that car. *She was headless*—the last thing she wanted was to be behind the wheel—but when that inconsiderate driver ran away in terror, what was a poor headless woman to do? She had to drive the car if she was ever going to make it home.

What's so awful about it? Why would you deny a cold lonely soul the right to slip into their home in the middle of the night and have a nice long talk with their family? Surely you would be thrilled to wake up one night to find your own dear sweet grandmother, whom you haven't seen for so many years, suddenly there beside your bed, smiling that wise grin of the dead. No doubt she's often thought of paying you a surprise visit (or at least that's what she told me).

The fact that more and more of the dead have been returning home should be a clear indication to you that your newspaper ought to be publishing more articles of interest to the dead.

Perhaps a story on facial creams Maybe a whole section devoted to death-styles of the rich and famous.

But all you seem to dwell on is how, after we've risen, we attack the living, turning them into one of us. Surely you can't see any harm in that—after all, we're just doing what creatures do naturally: increasing our numbers. Who are you to deny us that simple right?

And by the way, we resent the way your newspaper, and others, has referred to us in such insensitive and cold ways. We are not "zombies," we are not "moldering bones." The correct term for describing us is quite simply the "Living Dead"—and should you continue to refer to us in such unkind and bigoted ways, you will most certainly be hearing from the International Association of Living Dead Persons (IALDP).

And now I would like to set the record straight on this business about us eating the brains of the living. Don't you see how ridiculous that sounds? Why on earth would a person who has risen from the grave want to eat a human brain (no matter how tasty and delectable it might be)? After spending all that time wasting away in the graveyard, don't you think we might have developed a craving for something better—like maybe a steak, or some Häagen-Dazs? And anyway, I'm sure you'll agree there are quite a few people out there who could do with having their brains eaten. Oh, there are quite a few brains I personally can think of that would not be missed. And yours is high on my list. In fact, it's on all our lists. (That is . . . it *would* be if we actually *did* eat brains, and I'm not admitting that we do.)

But what gets me most, sir, are your laughable articles that announce the doom of mankind, and how you cheer the military's pathetic attempts to stop us from populating the finer neighborhoods of Rancid Falls. Why is it that you never mention that *we* are becoming the majority population of this lovely town? In fact, the only empty neighborhood in town is the graveyard. The dead have no use for it anymore, as we've decided if we must return to ashes and dust, then we might as well live out our deaths in a comfortable home, spending eternity watching old reruns of "I Love Lucy" (which are certain to be on for all eternity).

In the end, sir, I'd like to remind you that in this world of five billion living, breathing people, *we* are the majority. We've been here longer than you have, we will be here after you're gone—and believe me when I tell you that we have all decided it's time to come back.

So when you hear that knock at your door this evening, and when you open it to reveal a hungry, grinning crowd, their heads tilted to one side in the dim streetlight, don't be afraid. It's only us.

BOY ON A STOOP

···

A row of abandoned tenements rotted on a neglected city block where few people had reason to tread. There were a million ways to get where you were going without passing down that ruined street; nevertheless, Martina took that path to school every day. The buildings had been that way for years, and Martina felt a strange sort of affinity toward them. In many ways, they were like her: ignored . . . forgotten . . . friendless. Nothing, not even a row of buildings, deserved to be that unloved—so she limped her way down the broken weed-choked pavement of the condemned street every day.

That's where she saw him.

He sat on the stoop of one of those empty buildings, halfway down the block. It was the only one without a board nailed over the entrance. There was no door, just a dark rectangular hole, rimmed in chiseled plaster. Like her, the boy on the stoop seemed thirteen. He had jet black hair and features so handsome she couldn't help but stare at him out of the corner of her eye. She could feel his eyes following her as well, and it embarrassed her—because no boys looked at her. More often than not, they just looked away. Martina's glasses were thick, and one eye was slightly clouded from a childhood accident involving a neighbor boy and a stick. Then of course there was that horrible leg brace she was forced to wear on her weak right leg. She had been self-conscious about both her eye and her leg for as long as she could remember, keeping to herself and shying away from other kids. She preferred sticking to her books, and her many collections.

So naturally when she noticed this handsome boy looking at her, her face went red, and she hobbled out of his sight as quickly as she could.

He was there again as she walked home that day, still sitting on that porch as if he had nothing better to do than calmly watch life pass on the city pavement before him—and he was there the next day too, and the next. Each time he followed her with his eyes as she passed, like a portrait that always seemed to stare at you, no matter where you stood. It was easy to deal with being invisible, but being *noticed*—that was something entirely different.

Did he look at everyone like that or was it only me? wondered Martina. She concluded that there must be something wrong with him in the head, otherwise why would he be looking at her?

Her parents were not problem solvers when it came to talking through Martina's troubles. Her father, who worked two jobs, was rarely home, and when he was home, he was too exhausted to take much time for her. Martina's mom, who worked at a day-care center, was always frazzled, and the last thing she wanted to hear at the end of the day was a child's voice—even her own child's. Still, Martina knew she tried her best to be a functional parent.

One night she approached her mom, who sat up in bed, reading a sappy romance novel. "Mom, am I a good person?" she asked.

Her mother answered without hesitation, "Of course you are, honey."

"Then why don't more people like me?"

This time her mother did hesitate and began to rub her forehead as if the question had given her a headache. "It's not that they don't like you," she answered, "it's that they don't *know* you. If you let people know you a little better, then they'll like you a whole lot."

It was easy for her mother to say, but it just didn't work that way at school. There was a cruel pecking order in junior high, and once you found yourself at the bottom, the other kids wouldn't let you rise above it.

But the boy on the stoop wasn't a classmate. He didn't know her place in the pecking order.

Martina knew these were dangerous thoughts, because they filled her with the kind of hope that could be her ruin. So she returned to her room and tried to drive thoughts of the boy out of her mind. She read a book, recatalogued her various collections—rare coins, stamps, even exotic insects, pinned and labeled in a glass case. But not even her insect collection could keep thoughts of the boy away. In the end, she gave up, and closed the case on her tiny impaled bugs, locking it with a shiny silver key. She wished she could lock away her thoughts of the boy as easily.

* * *

The following Monday, a wind blew through the city, marking the arrival of fall. The leaves had already turned and were dropping to the pavement, where they would soon dry into brittle brown shells crunching underfoot. Martina wore a coat that was too heavy and out of style as she left for school.

When she peered down the boy's street, she could see him sitting on the porch again, leaning back on his elbows, relaxed and calm—such a stark contrast to the tension of the city. She approached him at a slow, steady pace, trying to hide her limp as best she could. Then, when she was in range, she turned to him—looking at him directly, rather than sneaking a glance. He smiled at her and she felt trapped in his deep green eyes. Her heart pounded a mysterious rhythm in her chest—a rhythm of fear and wonderful anticipation—because she knew that today she would say something to him.

But instead she gagged on the gum she was chewing and launched into a coughing fit.

"Are you all right?" he asked, getting up and taking a step closer to her.

Feeling like an imbecile, Martina cleared her lungs with a strong solid cough. The gum flew out and became one with the rest of the muck on the broken sidewalk. "I'm fine," she said.

"Good," said the boy. "I wouldn't want you to die. Not here on the sidewalk, anyway."

There was an uncomfortable moment, so Martina tried to fill it. "Don't you ever go to school?" she blurted out and immediately realized how nasty she must have sounded.

She thought he might make a nasty comment back to her, and that would end it forever. But instead he just kept smiling. "I get tutoring at home," he answered.

Now that she had the chance to study his face, she could see how irresistibly perfect it was. It should be illegal, she thought, for a face to be that perfect. He seemed smart too. Not just smart, but sharp. Sharp as a blade.

"What's your name?" he asked her.

"Martina."

"I'm Forest." He held out his hand, and as Martina reached forward to shake it, she dropped her books. They clattered on the cracked stoop and lay splayed and limp, like accident victims, on the sidewalk.

Martina quickly knelt to pick them up, but her brace didn't afford her such quick movements. Forest helped her, and when the books had all been collected she found herself sitting beside him on the stoop, like it was the most natural thing in the world.

"Why do you sit here?" she asked him.

Forest shrugged. "It's where I live."

Martina looked up at the ugly tenement. Five floors of windows, either broken or boarded over, graffiti scrawled on the soot-stained bricks—and if she listened, Martina imagined she could hear the scuttle of rats. "How very sad for you," said Martina.

He gave her his strange enigmatic smile again, and it penetrated her like a sudden blast of radiation. "It's not what you think," he said. "Would you like to see?" He gestured toward the entrance.

Martina turned to look into it. It was a dark cavity, and the wind echoed inside it, making it sound as if it were breathing. A heavy vine grew out of the darkness disappearing off the edge of the stoop, and she wondered what could possibly grow in a place like that.

"Uh . . . I'll be late for school," she answered and stood up, suddenly afraid of his friendship, and the place in which he lived.

He grabbed one of her books before she hurried off. "Maybe I can read this," he suggested. "And the next time you come we can talk about it together."

She nodded, feeling her familiar shyness closing up her throat so she couldn't speak. Then she turned and hurried down the street and around the corner to school.

As luck was no friend of Martina's, it turned out the book he borrowed, *Oddities of Nature*, was the subject of an oral report she was supposed to give that day. Still, she was glad that he took it . . . because it was one of her favorites, and when she worked up the nerve to walk down his street again, they'd have a lot to talk about.

"It doesn't make sense," she told her mother over dinner that night. "He's living in an abandoned building, but he says he has tutors."

Tonight her mom rubbed the back of her neck, instead of her forehead, which meant that her usual sinus headache had been replaced by her biweekly migraine. "Maybe we should talk to the police about him," she said, trying to hide the suspicion in her voice. "He could be a runaway."

Martina fiddled with the spaghetti on her plate. "If he's a runaway, he wouldn't be sitting out there like that, for the whole world to see."

"Well, whatever he is, I'd leave him alone if I were you."

Her mother's words lingered for the rest of the night, like the heavy taste of her over-spiced pasta. Her mom had always pushed Martina to make more friends, but at the same time injected her with a heavy dose of paranoia. Here was someone who seemed to welcome her friendship. Was she going to throw that away? As Martina prepared for bed, she studied her plain face in the bathroom mirror and wondered what the boy on the stoop saw when he looked at her that could possibly make him smile.

"It's a really interesting book," said Forest as they sat together after school the next day. Always on the stoop—never moving from the stoop. Together they flipped through the pages of *Oddities of Nature.* "It's full of weird things," said Forest.

"I know, isn't it great?" Martina flashed him a rare smile.

They turned to a page that featured a bird with both of its eyes on the same side of its head, then Forest pointed out his favorite—a frog that could freeze solid as a rock, but would come back to life when you defrosted it. Martina turned to a dog-eared page toward the back of the book.

"This is my favorite," she said. "The anglerfish."

The picture showed a strange-looking thing with small eyes, sharp teeth, and a wormlike stalk growing out of its forehead. "It hides behind rocks, or in the dirt," Martina explained, "so passing fish only see its stalk. The fish think it's a worm and try to munch on it, then the anglerfish jumps out and munches on *them.*"

Forest took a long look at her. "You really like strange things, huh?"

"Yeah," she said excitedly. "I collect them—strange coins, strange stamps—I even have a whole case full of strange bugs."

"You're not like the other girls," said Forest, never taking his eyes off her.

Martina looked away. "Are there lots of other girls that you talk to?"

"A few," said Forest, "but you're the most fun."

Martina couldn't look at him. She blushed. It was as if he

knew exactly what to say, exactly what she wanted to hear. When she dared to glance up at him again, he was grinning mischievously.

"I'll bet I can show you something weird you've never seen before!"

Martina closed the book. "What?"

He stood up, taking her hand, and moved her toward the dark peeling hole of the dead tenement building. Martina grabbed the rusting iron railing of the stoop, not letting herself be dragged in.

She thought of all the things her mother had told her about strangers—and all the warnings she had heard in school, ever since an eighth-grade girl had vanished the week before.

"It's okay," said Forest in the softest of voices, "you can trust me."

Somehow she felt certain that she could—that this boy would never do anything to harm her. And besides, everyone was sure that missing girl had just run away.

Martina loosened her grip on the rusted iron railing and let herself be led into the dank, decaying building.

Forest led her through the dismal building, following the trail of that long, thick vine that grew out the front door. Around her, the mildewed paper peeled in thick layers, and the termite-eaten wooden floors felt soft beneath her feet. Then he led her through a back door, into paradise.

In the city, most low-rise buildings faced back to back, and between them one could usually find a courtyard. Those narrow brick courtyards rarely saw the sun and were usually filled with weeds and trash. This hidden courtyard, however, surrounded on all sides by condemned buildings, held a garden.

Martina had read a book called *Lost Horizon* about a beautiful, magical place in the midst of snow-covered mountains. If there could be such a place in a concrete and steel city, then this was it. She had never seen trees ánd plants so beautiful—wide leaves dense and green, flowers blooming with every color of the rainbow. They all seemed to sway in the breeze. They seemed to gently reach toward her. Everywhere else in the city, leaves were turning, and trees were dying for the winter, but not here. This was a lush urban jungle. Barely able to catch her breath, she touched a large purple petal that felt like silk.

"But . . . how?"

"Must be an underground spring," suggested Forest, "or maybe just a broken hot-water pipe. Anyway, it's here."

She explored the dense garden with Forest, and he explained the many plants: one that only opened up in twilight and let off a rich blue light; another that had large round seeds embedded in its branches that looked like eyes, the same shade of green as his. Martina could swear she had seen one of them opening and closing.

It was then that Martina finally began to feel just a bit apprehensive. It was getting late; the courtyard had fallen deep into shadow, and the sun had left the sky. The afternoon had quickly become dusk.

"I'm glad," said Forest, "that you're not afraid. The others were all afraid."

There were too many things wrong with this picture. Martina knew just about all of the oddities creation had spat out—but none of the plants here were familiar at all.

And then there was the vine.

Down every path, that singular vine grew, ropy and dense. She followed it with her eyes to find where it ended, for it no longer grew through the door and into the tenement. Now it looped back into the garden, as if someone had moved it. At last she traced a path to its end. It only took a moment for her to realize the truth—and exactly what it meant.

With the sun gone from the sky, a huge leafy pod, two stories tall, had opened up in the southern corner of the garden—and inside was a flower a perfect shade of ocean blue, with a dozen soft petals each as large as her hand.

"Would you like to pick it?" asked Forest.

Martina looked at him sadly. "Are you my friend?" she asked him.

"Yes, Martina," he answered. "We're friends to the end."

Martina looked at the beautiful flower, and at the beautiful boy, then she reached down and lifted up the heavy green vine. As she held it, she could clearly see how it grew right into the base of his spine, like a tail—or more like an umbilical cord. "I knew you were special," she said to him, her voice barely a whisper. "But I didn't know how special."

The truth was, there was only one plant in here; it just had many different faces. Whether it evolved from the slime of the city, or whether it came here from someplace else, it thrived, like an anglerfish.

This handsome, charming boy was merely the worm to lure its prey.

She was terrified now, but told herself that she didn't care—that her fear didn't matter. Something as beautiful as this garden, as beautiful as *him*, deserved to live ... even if it meant that she had to die. There was almost something soothing and comforting to being devoured by this strange, exotic creature. Becoming a part of it.

Forest took her cold hands in his. "I need you to pick the flower, Martina ... Please."

Gently he guided her toward the large lovely leafed pod in the corner of the garden that loomed like a giant cavern. As they drew closer, she could see thick, black thorns, like jagged teeth, hidden beneath the leaves. "We'll be together forever," whispered Forest, "and you'll never feel lonely ever again."

She would have let him throw her inside—she wasn't afraid to die. But she was afraid of pain. In the end it was that fear that drove her to action.

Those thorns would hurt more than the teeth of a shark.

Just as Forest gave her one final push toward the open mouth of the cavern, Martina dug in her heels, reached up, and tore off one of the cavern's tooth-thorns. With a rush of air, the giant mouth snapped shut on the hem of her dress.

"No!" she screamed. The green cavern opened its mouth once more, baring its black teeth, and the entire thing lurched closer. It clamped down on her leg—she could feel the pain shoot up her whole body. Forest backed away, his vine trailing into the thick underbrush.

"I'm sorry," he said. "I'm sorry, Martina." The giant jaws opened once more and chomped down again, getting more of her.

But it wasn't over yet. The thorn in her hand was sharp as a carving knife. She knew she couldn't fight the thing trying to eat her, so she reached out and grabbed the vine—Forest's vine—and she sliced into it.

"Don't!" screamed Forest, in a sudden terror more powerful than her own.

She felt the jaw behind her loosen its grip on her leg. She sliced into the vine again. Around her all the leaves, all the flowers, began to rustle and shake. She pulled on the vine, and Forest fell over. Then at last she found the thinnest part of his umbilical cord, jammed the knife into it, and sliced through it again and again, until she had cut it in two, separating Forest now and forever from the plant.

The boy-thing screamed, and his chilling wail echoed off the brick walls of the condemned buildings around them. Then she felt the pressure on her leg release. The leaves around her wilted and dropped, the flowers disappeared into their buds, and in a moment all was silence.

She pried open the jaws of the cavernous plant. She was bleeding, but not as badly as she had thought. It was her horrible curse of a leg brace that had saved her. The thing couldn't bite through the steel! She pulled herself free, and the dead green jaws closed with a sickening *thwump*.

She went over to Forest, who lay on the ground, as still as the rest of the garden, not breathing. But then, he had never breathed in the first place, had he?

She cradled his head in her arms, brushed his dark hair out of his face, and with tears in her eyes, she kissed him. Then she grabbed him by the arms and dragged him across the dark ground of the dead garden.

A few weeks later they tore the whole block down and found just what they expected to find in the courtyard—the dry, crumbled remains of dead city weeds, although the weeds here seemed to have grown much thicker than most other places.

Since that day, Martina always left for school early—but she didn't go straight to school. Instead, she went to the basement of her apartment building. There was a storage room down there, a room that few people knew about, and no one— not even the building manager—ever went into. It was one of the many forgotten places of the city.

Inside the claustrophobic room sat a beautiful boy with sparkling green eyes. His eyes stared up fearfully at Martina as she entered.

"So you're finally awake," said Martina. "You've been unconscious for over a month."

Beside the boy was a clay pot filled with rich potting soil, and above him hung a fluorescent grow-light that made his soft skin look blue. He was very thin, but Martina knew that would be only temporary. The boy shifted to reveal the knotty vine growing from the small of his back and into the clay pot, where it had taken root. Martina poured in a pitcher of water spiked with a healthy dose of Miracle-Gro. Then she took a hamster from her pocket and released it on the ground.

"You're going to be fine," Martina told him calmly. "I have a green thumb, you know. I'll nurse you back to health."

A small tuber had already grown from the pot, and at its end was a fist-sized pod. The hamster sniffed at the pod; the pod opened and snapped closed around the hamster without a sound. The boy barely seemed to notice. Eating was an automatic response.

"Eventually you'll need larger things," Martina whispered, "but I'll take care of that too. I'll take care of everything."

The boy opened his mouth to speak, but his voice was raspy from his many weeks of sleep. "Why?" he asked. "Why have you done this?"

"Because you're my friend," she answered, happy and in control. "You're *my* friend . . . and you'll talk with me, and you'll play games with me, and we'll have good times together for the rest of our lives, won't we, Forest?"

And as she said it, she brought out a huge pair of gardening shears and set them gingerly on a shelf.

Forest shuddered at the sight of the shears. "Yeah," he said in weak but terrible dread. "Yeah, uh . . . it'll be . . . great."

Martina smiled again as she gazed lovingly at him, then she

turned and limped out the door. With a shiny silver key, she locked all three deadbolts behind her.

Outside, the day was cold, but that didn't matter, because now something warm and wonderful filled Martina's heart. How good it was to be blessed with a friend like Forest.

RETAINING
WALLS

••

On a morning full of cold clouds, my father sweeps me out of bed and into his pickup truck—as if I have nothing better to do with my Sunday than to sit at his work site and watch grown men play with blocks.

"Have fun," says Mom, as if that were possible. "Don't stay out too late."

My dad smiles at her and waves as we drive off. It's the warmest gesture he can give her, now that they're divorced. Dad shoves a doughnut and a juice box into my hands as a makeshift breakfast, then he spirits me away to his work.

Big walls. That's my father's specialty. He built his first wall when he was nineteen, in the basement of an old house. From what I heard, a mudslide had caved in the weak basement wall, and Dad had gone in with Grandpa to build a strong retaining wall to hold the mud back where it should be. Thing is, Grandpa died halfway through the job, and Dad had to finish it alone. Since then, he hasn't stopped building walls.

As we drive, I can see my father's anticipation building. He likes his work—it invigorates him. You could say he lives for it, as if what he does has an importance beyond what I can measure. I always thought him small-minded to find such pleasure in the placement of stone. But then who am I to talk? I spend hours in front of a TV screen playing video games. I guess the best I can say is that what he does is *constructive*, in the literal sense of the word.

My ears pop, and I realize we are heading out of town, up into the hills. Out of the window, through the early morning haze, I can see our town below us, a grid stretching toward the horizon.

"Nice view from here," he says. "Even better where we're going." He grins at me with a glimmer in his eye. "You'll like this one, Memo."

He's the only one I still let call me Memo, or even Guillermo. To most everyone else, I'm Billy.

"I thought we were going to work on my pitching today."

"This is an important job," he reminds me. "I'm on a tight schedule. We'll do it next week," he says.

Which is what he said last week, and the week before that. I only get to see him on Sundays—you'd think he'd be able to take that day off to spend with me, but instead of making time for me, he just squeezes me into what he's already doing, whether I fit or not.

We head up a dusty dirt path that seems to be made for things with feet rather than wheels. The cab of the pickup bounces, and I can feel the doughnut and juice sloshing around in my stomach like surf in a storm. Finally we pull off to the side of the dirt road, in the middle of nowhere, with a cliff to the right of us and a steep slope looming above us to the left. "We're here," he tells me.

"Here, where?"

"You'll see," he answers. Then he begins to climb up the side of the slope. I follow, feeling sleep still gnawing at my bones.

As we come over the top of the hill, I can see half a dozen workers—Dad's crew—busying themselves dusting and buffing the large boulders on a plateau. I see no house, no construction site. Nothing but a mountain.

"What's the deal here?" I ask him. "Where's the wall?"

"We're doing boulderscape today," he answers.

I know about boulderscape. No matter how much I've tried to ignore my father's work, some of it sneaks into my head. He's done whole patios and pools that look just like natural rock formations, when in reality it's just mortar over chicken wire.

"Can you tell which is real and which I put in?" he asks me, proud of his accomplishment.

As I look around, I can't tell—but the thing is, what's the sense of putting fake rocks in the middle of real ones? I mean, usually it's rich people who put in boulderscape. They have my dad build pools, and waterfalls, and hot tubs in fake caves to impress their friends and neighbors. But out here, the only things to impress are coyotes and rattlesnakes.

He leads me to a sheer rock face looming above the plateau; a dark granite mountainside that must have been here for eons.

"The real rock starts about ten feet up," Dad tells me.

I stare at him dumbfounded. "You mean . . . ?"

"That's right," he says. "This stone face is a retaining wall. I built it!"

I shake my head, not getting it. "But . . . can't a mountain retain itself?"

Dad raises his eyebrows. "Apparently not," he says, then goes off to discuss the progress with his crew.

As I look around, I find a small spot that hasn't been finished: a patch of gray mortar and chicken wire in the midst of the boulders and evergreens, like a hole in reality.

Humberto, Dad's best craftsman, spreads mortar across the chicken wire, hiding its fine metallic honeycomb.

Now I begin to notice the breeze. It's been chilly, and breezy, but up here, on this strange plateau, it feels different from the dry mountain cold elsewhere. It feels damp—and there's something about the smell. I take a deep breath and have a sudden flashback to a vacation we had years ago, in Florida. I don't understand why at first, but then the reason strikes me. It smells like beach. It smells like the ocean.

I hold out my hand to feel the breeze and notice that it's not blowing down the mountain, but blowing up—as if it's blowing out of the ground—I can feel it against my palm!

I turn to see that the workers all carry caulking guns and are going around the base of the boulders, filling in the cracks with thick cream, the kind of stuff you put around a bathtub to keep it from leaking.

I kneel down next to Humberto, and for an instant I think I see something through the wire framing of the boulder. I see a greenish-blue light. I see mist and clouds. I get dizzy, as if suddenly I'm looking down from a great height.

"Whoa!" I say, grabbing onto a boulder for balance.

"What's the matter?" asks my father, coming up behind me.

"I don't know . . . I think there's a cave down there . . . a pretty deep one."

"Really!" he says.

"Yeah! I tried to look into it but—"

"Did it look back?" my father asks.

"Huh?"

He grins. "Your grandfather used to say that when you look into an abyss, the abyss looks into *you*."

The thought gives me the shivers. I glance back down to peer in the hole, but Humberto has already smeared a thick patch of mortar over the chicken wire.

There are lots of reasons to build a wall, I suppose. To mark off territory; to hide things you don't want to deal with; to keep things in; to keep things out. To repair the damage. There must be an awful lot of damage to repair, because my dad's beeper always goes off, calling him to new jobs—sometimes halfway around the world. That's how good he is.

On Monday morning, I ask my mom about my father, and walls.

Mom doesn't answer right away. She slowly pours herself a cup of black coffee, dumping in a heaping teaspoon of sugar. Then she weighs her response very carefully.

"Your father's walls are special," she says. "Not just his walls, but his patios as well."

"And his boulderscapes?" I add.

She nods. "There are very few masons in the world who can do work like your father," she tells me. "He's a true artist."

"Then why did you divorce him?" I ask her, point-blank. It's a question I've never had the guts to speak aloud before.

Mom takes a long sip of her sweet, steaming coffee. "I don't know if this will make sense to you, Billy, but when someone is as good as your father is ... sometimes they *become* their work."

"You mean that talking to him is like talking to a wall?" I suggest.

She laughs out loud. "Something like that," she says, although I can tell there is much more to it.

I'm about to tell her about the mountain boulderscape and

how strange it all seemed. I open my mouth to talk—but before I can, my hand saves me, by shoving a spoonful of cereal in my mouth and shutting me up.

Next Sunday I'm awake before dawn, waiting for my father to arrive. Until last week, I had never looked closely enough at my dad's work to notice, or care, about what he was doing— but last week's excursion has lingered with me. I can't wait to see what job we're working on today.

He picks me up at the usual time. Six o'clock A.M.

"Are we headed to the mountains today?" I ask.

He shakes his head. "Nope, we're finishing up a wall downtown."

"What kind of wall?" I ask.

"The usual."

Half an hour later, we reach the deserted business district, where nobody in their right mind comes on a Sunday. We enter a twenty-story building. The wall is on the fifteenth floor, in the offices of Moreland and Beck, Attorneys-at-Law.

The second the elevator doors open on fifteen, we are blasted by a breath of hot air from down the hall. And as we approach the offices of Moreland and Beck, the heat rises a degree with every footfall.

"Haven't they ever heard of an air conditioner?" I say, but even as I say it, I can feel the cooler air blowing from the vents above, fighting a losing battle to control the temperature.

In the law office, a spongy gray carpet has been rolled back, revealing the concrete beneath, and at the far end is a twenty-foot-wide stone-block wall where a window should be.

"That's a weird place for a wall," I tell my father.

"Walls go wherever you need them," says Dad.

As I get closer, the heat becomes more intense. My jacket, which had been protecting me from the cold morning, suddenly seems ridiculous. I take it off and throw it over a chrome-backed chair. Humberto and the others drill holes in the existing cement floor and insert heavy three-quarter-inch rebar—those heavy iron bars that hold walls together. Seems to me that they're spacing those bars closer than they usually do. I can see that they're building a second wall of cinder block, in front of the finished stone one.

"Two walls?" I ask my father. "Isn't that a waste?"

"Believe me, it's not," he says. He puts a mortar trowel into my hand, then brings me a bucket of mortar. "It's about time you started to learn the trade," he tells me. "Our family has been masons for as long as anyone can remember. It would be a shame if that tradition ended with me."

I hold the tool in my hand, feeling clumsy, like I have no right to use it, as if it were a medical instrument and I was about to perform surgery.

"You spread," he tells me. "I'll lay the stone."

And so I join him and his workers building the second wall in the oppressive heat. The sweat beads on my face and rolls down my cheeks. I lick my lips and can taste its saltiness.

"Very good," he tells me as I spread the mortar as smooth as cake icing. "You're a natural. Someday you'll be building walls better than all of us."

The idea doesn't thrill me, but it doesn't sicken me either. Not if the walls I build are like this.

There are a lot of things I should be asking my father now. I should question him about this steaming wall—about the mountainside the week before. But the thing is, communication has never been a family strong point. We've spent most of our lives holding things back and keeping problems out. It's hard to fight a lifetime of training, so I don't ask him the questions I want to. Instead I just spread the gritty gray cement and watch as Dad piles on the heavy blocks.

I keep my eyes focused on that first wall. I can feel the heat pulsing from it, like highway blacktop in summer. I want to know what's behind it. I reach forward to see just how hot it is, touching my fingertips against it.

"Memo! No!"

Too late. I touch it for an instant, and that instant is too long. I draw my hand back reflexively, feeling the shock of the burn even before the pain, and when the pain comes, it flows down from my fingertips in angry waves. I refuse to scream. I grit my teeth, and the scream comes out as a moaning hiss.

Dad grabs me and pulls me away.

"Humberto, the first aid!" he orders.

He leads me to an outer room, which is a bit cooler, but not by much.

As Dad tends to my throbbing fingertips, I can feel the pain turning into tears, which roll down my face, mixing with my sweat. Hanging on the wall around me, I can see the fire-suits they must have used to put up that first wall. *What's behind there?* I want to ask. *Why did you have to build this wall?* But I don't say a thing. I just look away as my father gently bandages my hand, and I watch as his crew rolls out thick insulation as pink as cotton candy to fill the space between the first and second wall.

Dad keeps me late tonight. Maybe he just doesn't want to face Mom's wrath when he brings me home with bandaged fingers. We grill burgers and I eat with my left hand instead of my right.

Away from his work there isn't much he knows how to say.

"How's school?" he asks. Fine, I tell him.

"How's baseball?" he asks. Fine, I tell him.

And in a few moments, there's nothing he can think of to ask me. But rather than letting the ball drop into an uncomfortable and distant place, I start to mention things I'm sure will keep him talking.

"What's the hardest part about building walls?" I ask.

His ears perk up with the question. "The hardest part is figuring out how to build them strong enough."

"Strong enough for what?"

"So that nothing can ever break through," he answers. "Strong enough so that the wall will last forever and ever."

I grin. "C'mon, Dad," I tell him. "Nothing lasts forever."

He thinks about that. "I guess you're right," he admits. "If things lasted forever, I wouldn't have any work."

He takes a bit of his burger and ponders me while he chews.

"I want to show you something before I take you home," he announces, then he stands up, grabbing his jacket. "Let's go."

I have no idea what he has in mind, but I go along, not daring to ask what it is.

An abandoned house sits at the end of an abandoned road, at the edge of Dad's neighborhood. Broken windows stare at me like eyes, their tattered shades like drooping eyelids. They gaze out with the indifferent look of the dead.

Dad opens his car door and steps out. I follow. The sun is already gone from the horizon, and what little glow remains will fade in a few minutes. I think I know what this house must be—and I have no desire to see it—but I can't tell Dad, so I force my feet to follow him to the front door.

There's a padlock on the termite-gnawed wood of the door, but it's easily kicked in with his strong foot.

Inside the empty dwelling we go, then down a rickety set of basement steps, to the only thing in the house that is sturdy.

The wall.

It's a simple thing, made of red brick, completely out of

place in this decaying home. About as out of place as the hot stone slab in the glass office building.

The ground beneath us is covered with two inches of water. A hundred rains from a dozen rainy seasons have taken their toll. Around us are cinder blocks, and bags of old mortar piled on a table, as if more work had been planned but got abandoned like the house.

"Every mason has his first wall," says Dad. "This was mine. I was nineteen," he reminds me. "I didn't know what I wanted to do with my life. And after seeing how hard my own father worked, I didn't think building walls would be for me—until this one." He touched his hand against a rough brick, feeling the troughs in the crusty mortar. "With each brick I laid in this wall, the clearer it became that this was my calling, too. So I learned to love it."

I can't read the look on his face—which is no surprise. If I could read faces, I probably would have known my parents were getting divorced before they sprang it on me that day.

"It's just a wall," I remind my dad. "There's nothing really special about it."

"Go up and touch it," he says to me, like a challenge. So I take a step closer, and as I do, I begin to feel dizzy. I suddenly reach forward, as if I'm falling down, but I don't hit the ground. Instead my hands slap against the wall, and I feel pain shoot through my burned fingertips. The hard, cold brick seems to have a gravity about it, pulling me closer—and there's a faint vibration in the icy brickwork.

I put my ear against it. They say you can hear the ocean when you put your ear against a seashell, but I've never heard of hearing something when you listen to brick—and yet I do. It's a hollow sound, cold and lonely, punctuated by an occasional rumble that sounds like a growl, and a *pfft-pfft-pfft*, like the flapping of bat wings.

I push myself away from the wall, stepping back until I am far enough away not to feel off balance.

"What's behind that wall, Dad?"

Dad rubs his eyes and bites his lip.

"Your grandfather," he says.

When I get home that night, I don't tell my mother what happened to my hand. No matter how much she asks, I just tell her it's nothing and yell at her to leave me alone. Eventually she stops asking. I spend the next day out so I don't have to talk to her about it, and then stay late at school through the week so I don't have to answer to her at all. Funny how when you don't talk about things, the easier they are not to deal with. I figure my head is about the best retaining wall there is, when it comes to holding things back . . .

. . . but by the end of the week, my little mental dike has sprung a leak.

Your grandfather's behind that wall.

It's a strange thing to say, even for my father. I had half expected him to laugh after he said it, like it was a joke—but he didn't laugh. He just climbed silently up the steps and out of the old house.

The thing is, my dad's a very literal person—he doesn't think poetically. He thinks in solid chunks of reality. His mind works in brick and concrete—which means that when he says my grandfather is behind that wall, he means that my grandfather *is* behind that wall.

I'm terrified that I might actually ask him about it when I see him again. It will take all my strength to just go on like everything's normal. Whatever work site he brings me to, certainly there'll be more weirdnesses to occupy my imagination. Still, the wall in the abandoned house is like a brick in my head. What's behind that wall? What's behind all of the walls my father builds? It occurs to me that he's never brought me to a wall when he first starts building it—only when the job is almost done. When it's too late to see the other side.

On Saturday night, I get a call from Dad. Apparently he and Mom have been talking in secret—as usual—making decisions about my life without involving me.

"Memo, your mom and I have decided that it's best if we don't spend Sundays together anymore."

All I can do is stutter and sputter like an idiot.

"My work sites are dangerous. More dangerous than you know," he tells me. "It's not a place for a kid."

"But . . . but I'll be careful!" I insist. "Please! I *want* to come. I want to know about the walls . . . I want to watch you build them." And then, because I have nothing else to lose, I say, "I want to know what you meant about Grandpa . . ."

I hear him take a deep breath on the other end of the line. "I was wrong, Memo," he tells me. "You shouldn't be putting up walls all your life like me. You should find something *you* love!"

"But I want to be with you!" I scream at him, the tears exploding from my eyes like they did the day he moved out. "When will I get to see you now?"

"Vacations," he says. "Summer, maybe."

But the thing is, he doesn't take vacations—and if he won't take me to his sites anymore, then I'll never get to see him again. That's what he means. We both know it.

"Memo, my work is getting harder. More repairs—more emergency work. You understand, don't you?"

"You stink!" I tell him, and I hang up on him before he can say anything else.

From behind me I can hear my mom trying to talk to me gently, like she can wrap her arms around me and make everything all better. She must be crazy to think I have anything to say to her now.

She holds out her arms, but I push my way past her refusing to talk about it. If the only defense I have is closing myself off, I can do that just fine.

I go out to the garage, and there I find a pickax. It's heavy, but there's angry adrenaline rushing through my body now, and I can lift it onto my shoulder. I storm out of the house, ignoring my mother calling behind me. It's a long walk but I know where I'm going.

I push open the ruined door of the abandoned house. The floorboards creak beneath me, and a stair cracks under my weight as I go down into the dank, water-logged basement. A single clouded window sheds a feeble shaft of light upon the brick wall. I waste no time in thinking. If I think, I may find a reason to stop myself.

I swing the pickax high and smash it against the wall. Chunks of brick fly in all directions. It might be solid, but nothing lasts forever. I swing the pickax again, and again, until I've made a crater in its red face.

I *will* know what's behind there. I *will* know what my father has spent his life doing; what he locks behind the walls he builds. I don't care if I have to shatter every single wall to know—and if I come face-to-face with the grandfather I never knew behind this one, then that will be just fine with me.

Another swing, and another. The hollow noises beyond the wall seem to grow louder, until finally the pickax crashes through to the other side. I pull it out and hear a whistling of wind, sucking out through a hole the size of my fist. I swing again, to widen the hole.

The flapping sounds and growls are louder. I hear screeches now, awful high-pitched screeches. Those sounds ought to make me stop, but my mind is like a car speeding off a cliff. I can't stop my hand from swinging the ax.

"Memo! Memo, don't!"

It's my father. Mom must have called him and told him I ran out with the ax. It didn't take a genius to figure out where I had gone. I can hear him leaping down the stairs behind me, and I know he'll stop me. He'll patch up the hole and never talk about it, like it never happened. But I can't let him do that!

I raise the ax and give one final, powerful swing.

And the solid brick wall shatters like glass.

I can see the fracture lines spreading through the brick in all directions. Then the whistling wind becomes a gale, and I feel myself being dragged forward toward a gaping hole six feet wide.

At the lip of the hole, I feel something sharp against my gut. I've been snagged by a piece of the reinforcing steel bar, sticking out from the brickwork. I grab onto it, to keep myself from falling into the hole.

"Memo, give me your hand."

My father reaches for me desperately, his sturdy hand stretching out for my madly wriggling fingers until he clasps them—but at that same moment I feel something at my feet, and I look into the pit.

In the cold, murky darkness, some creature is moving—a terrible living unknown, with beady, hungry eyes, and reptilian wings. It opens a tooth-filled mouth and nips off the rubber tip of my running shoe, just missing my toes. Then it disappears with a flap of its veiny wings into the darkness, like a great white shark testing its prey before the kill. For an instant, as the mist is torn by its wake, I see a tortured landscape of nightmare trees and screaming skies of black ice. I feel my grip beginning to slip.

"Don't look, Memo!" warns my father. In an instant he is

there with me, clinging onto the heavy steel bar, which suddenly seems as frail as wire—just as the unknown beast returns, its jaws spread wide.

My father swings his fist at it, but the thing clamps down on his wrist. I can feel his pain as he screams. Clinging to the rebar, I kick the creature over and over in its awful eye, jamming it with my heel, until it finally lets my father go and flaps away into deeper, colder regions of miscreation.

We pull ourselves out of the hole, tumbling onto the wet floor of the old basement.

Behind us is the wall—or what's left of it—and beyond the hole, the awful landscape swarms with things too strange and savage to be named.

I take off my jacket and wrap it tightly around my father's mangled hand.

"The hole . . ." he hisses. "We can't leave the hole."

On the table rest the old, forgotten bags of mortar. I hurry to them, tearing them open and letting the dusty mixture pour into the ankle-deep water at our feet. Then I grab the abandoned cinder blocks one by one and move them toward the hole.

My father, unable to help, can only watch as I spread the mortar on thick with my hands and lay the cinder blocks on one by one.

There are no creatures near us now, but still I won't look into the hole again.

When you stare into an abyss, I think, *the abyss stares into you.*

"Your grandfather was working on this wall when he died," Dad says as I pile on another cinder block. "He had brought me here—to show me just what kind of work he did . . . but he looked too deeply into that place . . . and it swallowed him. I watched him fall, but there was nothing I could do. In the end, all I could do was finish the wall that he started."

I spread the mortar thick and slam down another block. In spite of the terror I know I should feel, something about laying those blocks calms me.

"I'm not living with Mom anymore," I tell Dad as I close off one world from another with the last heavy block. "I'm living with you."

My father nods, realizing my decision is final. "If that's what you want," he says.

I smooth the mortar between the blocks. I know that I won't speak of this night again. Not to Mom, not to Dad, not to anyone. I will hold it back. I will keep it in the dark—as Dad has kept dark the many strange places he's seen through the holes of the world.

And I, too, will build walls.

After seeing that other side, there's an acceptance and understanding in me now. I know what my life has to be.

I suppose there are three kinds of people in this world. Some people live their lives *around* the holes—never finding them, never even worrying about them. Their lives are full and happy. Then there are others who keep falling through those hidden gaps, into nightmares they never knew existed. I wouldn't want to be one of them.

And then there's a few like my dad and me; restless people who spend our lives plugging holes in the unfinished corners of creation and building walls to hold back all the things that must never be seen.

Perhaps there's more holes than can be patched in a lifetime. But I've got to live on the hope that maybe, just maybe, we'll get them all . . . and the abyss will never look into us again.

Where they came from . . .

• •

I am often asked where I get my ideas, so I thought I'd share the origins of the stories in *MindQuakes*.

Yardwork

I was giving a workshop at a school I was visiting. The task was to come up with an unlikely title, brainstorm story ideas, and then try to develop the most unlikely idea. The title we began with was "The Man Next Door." Someone suggested that he's burying something in his garden, and everyone tossed out the usual possibilities: His money, his family, his boss—and then someone shouted out "he's burying himself." The classroom laughed, but I thought the idea was just quirky enough to work. The question is, why would he do such a thing? My goal was to take a potentially morbid idea, and turn it into something as heartwarming as it was creepy.

Caleb's Colors

There's a painting in my living room by Eyvind Earle, a favorite artist of mine—a surrealistic landscape draped with a bough of leaves, redder than red. You can stare at its unearthly beauty for hours, and never get tired of it. It's as if you can walk right in. . . .

Ralphy Sherman's Jacuzzi of Wonders

My six-year-old son Brendan thinks the Loch Ness Monster is just about the coolest thing in the world, and can tell you all there is to know about it. Once, when we were all sitting in a particularly murky Jacuzzi, Brendan said, "I'll bet this Jacuzzi is about as cloudy as Loch Ness," and then he smiled, because we both knew it was going to end up as a story. As for Ralphy Sherman, he's the one and only character who appears in all of my books. Someday he'll get a book of his own.

Number 2

What if inanimate objects had hopes and dreams of their own, just like us? As I thought about that, it occurred to me that a classroom pencil led a pretty miserable life. Sharpened and gnawed on, then sharpened again. All the worse if you're a pencil with dreams of greatness.

The Soul Exchange

Ever since Veruca Salt went down the garbage shoot in Willy Wonka's factory, I've loved stories about unpleasant kids who got their just desserts. With that in mind, I wanted to see what would happen to a self-absorbed kid who found a way to trade in bodies as easily as people trade in cars. And what if our greedy kid found herself taken in a used car scam?

Damien's Shadow

I awoke one night to see a heavy tree branch casting a dark shadow on my wall. While the tree itself was unimpressive, the shadow of the branch made it look like a "hanging-tree," the kind they used to dispense justice in the old west. But a shadow was all you could hang from a shadow-limb, right? Then I began to wonder what would make someone want to hang a shadow? I was too spooked to sleep, so I got up and spent all night writing the story.

Terrible Tannenbaum

True story. Or at least part of it. A few years back, we had this unfortunate Christmas tree. It would loom all day long, then every night keel over, and shatter ornaments all over the piano. We had to string it up to our wall and upstairs banister in three places to keep it from falling. But this tree was like Houdini—because it pulled free from its bonds, and fell again. The kids were terrified of it—they kept looking at, afraid it might fall on them as they passed. They feared for Santa.

Dead Letter

With all the horror movies about the living-dead, it occurred to me that no one has ever come forward to complain about how the living-dead are portrayed in the media. After all, everyone else complains, why not them?

Boy on a Stoop

I saw this kid when I was in New York, sitting on the stoop of an abandoned building, like he belonged there. He was reading *Catcher in the Rye*. For some reason, it seemed downright creepy to me, and it stuck in my mind. Then, recently I read a book with my sons about strange sea creatures, like the angler-fish. I began to wonder what a creature that was angling after humans might have as its "worm." Well that all depends on what it's trying to catch. . . .

Retaining Walls

We recently had a patio put in our backyard—which is not as easy as it seems, I found out. Part of the job required putting up a retaining wall to hold back the hill from mudslides, earth-quakes, nuclear war and Alien invasions. Or so you would think, considering the amount of work that went into building the thing. With walls on the brain, I couldn't help but write this story!

N. S.

This book is over, but
the journey has only begun . . .

Destination: the twisted depths of your own brain.
Your ticket: your imagination.

MindQuakes is not a place you'll find on a map. It's not a journey that takes place on a road, but on a plane whose dimensions have neither substance nor depth. And yet it exists. You'll find it at the end of those jagged lines where reality splinters and disappears.

Want to ride along? Well, hop in. But remember: there is no speed limit on the highway through the mind. And no U-turns. So hold on tight.

Don't miss other titles in this exciting series from award-winner Neal Shusterman.